The Dead Heart

Also by Douglas Kennedy

Beyond The Pyramids
In God's Country
Chasing Mammon

The Dead Heart

Douglas Kennedy

A *Little, Brown* Book

First published in Great Britain by Little, Brown and Company 1994

Copyright © Douglas Kennedy 1994

The moral right of the author has been asserted.

Lines from 'The Ballad of the Green Berets' by Barry Allen Sadler and
Robin Moore are reproduced by permission of Peter Maurice Music Co Ltd,
London WC2H 0EA. Copyright © 1963, Music Music Music Inc, USA.

Lines from 'I Feel Pretty' by Bernstein and Sondheim are reproduced by
permission of Campbell Connelly & Co. Copyright © 1957 (renewed) Leonard
Bernstein and Stephen Sondheim Jalni Publications Inc, USA & Canadian
publisher. G Schirmer Inc, worldwide print rights and publisher rest of the world.
Campbell Connelly & Co Ltd, 8/9 Frith Street, London W1V 5TZ.
International Copyright secured. All Rights Reserved.

The extract on page vii is taken from Dunleavy, Maurice, *Stay Alive: a handbook
on survival*, AGPS Press, 1981. Commonwealth of Australia copyright © 1981
reproduced by permission.

Although every effort has been made to contact copyright holders of all material
used in this book the publishers would be pleased to hear from any copyright
holders whom we appear to have been unable to trace if their material appears in
this book.

A CIP catalogue record for this book
is available from the British Library.

ISBN 0 316 90947 5

Typeset by M Rules
Printed and bound in Great Britain by
Clays Ltd, St Ives plc

Little, Brown and Company (UK) Limited
Brettenham House
Lancaster Place
London WC2E 7EN

for Max Kennedy

'The lonely man in a strange environment is naturally
fearful.'

– from *Stay Alive* by Maurice Dunleavy:
An Australian government handbook on Outback survival.

part one

part one

one

I had never seen so many tattoos. Everybody in Darwin had one. Everybody in this bar had one – including the stripper who was dancing atop a makeshift stage, showing off the Red Admiral butterfly engraved on her left buttock.

I pegged her as a woman around thirty. She was one thin stripper – 99lbs, no chest, twiggy legs. And she looked seriously out of love with life – perhaps because she was paid to let a bunch of toxic bushmen look up her wazoo.

I'd walked into this joint in time to catch the start of her act. It was a big bleak cavern of a place. Behind the bar was a collection of steel refrigerator doors with large handles – the same kind of doors that you'd find in a mortuary. Each door gave way to a six-foot-deep ice-chest crammed with tins of lager, and the barmen all greeted you with the same question – 'Can of piss?' – for this was a dump which only served beer.

Directly opposite the bar was a piece of plywood balanced on two tea-chests. As a scratchy recording of 'Fun, Fun, Fun' by The Beach Boys blared over a loudspeaker, the stripper hit the stage. She was dressed like a no-taste housewife ready for a day at the beach: a bikini, a wide-brimmed straw hat, dark glasses and a beachball. She used this beachball as a kind of warm-up prop, trying to establish a rapport with her public by tossing it out into the sea of distended abdomens which had crowded around the platform. But her public tossed the ball back and roared at her to get on with the job. Her face tightened into a 'fuck you' grimace as off went the hat, off went the shades, off went the bikini top and bottom. Then down she went on her back to begin a series of leg splits. The crowd hooted their approval.

The guy sitting next to me nudged my arm.

'Know what she puts me in mind of?' he said. 'The San Andreas fault.'

'No shit?' I said, noticing that the dude had a furry spider tattooed across one bicep. I started making a move for another bar stool, but the guy proffered his hand.

'Jerry Watts,' he said. A geek with a blond crew-cut, buck teeth, a moustache in need of fertilizer and that goddamn tattoo. I reluctantly gripped the outstretched paw.

'Nick Hawthorne.'

'You from my part of the world, friend?'

'Yeah, I'm a Yank.'

'Whereabouts?'

'Maine.'

'Fuckin' Maine-iac, huh?'

'Something like that.'

'Me, I'm Motown. *Dee*-troit. Though I was stationed down in 'Bama before the army shipped me out here. You military, Nick?'

'Nah, civilian.'

4

'The fuck you doin' up here? Only Americans I ever meet in Darwin are Army.'

'I'm just passing through.'

'Where to?'

'South.'

'South. Shit, all you can do in Darwin is go south, 'cause this is about as north as it gets round here. Where you tryin' to head to?'

'Not sure. Perth, maybe.'

'Perth, *maybe*? You know how far Perth is from here?'

'About two thousand miles.'

'Damn right it is. And you know what you're gonna find between here and Perth? Two thousand miles of *nothing*. And I'm talkin' serious, four-hours-to-the-next-shithouse nothing. You ever been down that road before?'

I shook my head.

'Well, hope you got a taste for the weird, 'cause you're gonna meet a lot of it. And when the going gets weird out there, the weird turn pro. Believe me, I know what I'm saying.'

'You seem to know a great deal about a great many things.'

'Guess I do, guess I do. 'Course, I've only been there once before, when we were on manoeuvres last year. But I tell you true: I've never seen more *nothing* in my life . . . Bartender, couple of cold ones here . . .'

'I really shouldn't . . .'

'You runnin' off somewhere?'

'Not really . . . It's just . . . I only arrived last night and I'm still a bit jet-lagged, so I'm trying to take it easy on the beer.'

'Hell, another brew or two ain't gonna kill you.'

Up on stage, the stripper turned her back to the crowd, then crouched down on all fours and stood on her head. The crowd broke into spontaneous applause.

'Now that's what I call a scenic view,' Jerry Watts said. 'Though if I were her old man, I'd fatten her up a bit, 'cause she's a little too scrawny for comfort, if you know what I mean.'

I stared into my can of Export and said nothing.

'You married, Nick?'

'No.'

'Never been down the aisle?'

'Never.'

'Me, I've been down there twice. Once when I was seventeen, then again at twenty-one. Now I'm based in Okinawa, Japan and I got me a cute little Filipina girlfriend. Name of Mamie. And I'm just thinkin' of marrying Mamie – though every time I come to Darwin for manoeuvres, I keep thinkin' I should land me one of these Aussie women, 'cause they are the most beautiful ballbusters on the planet. You ever boff one of 'em?'

'Can't say that I have.'

'Never boffed an Aussie, never been married . . . Man, you have led one sheltered life.'

'I suppose so.'

'You got a job?'

'Between 'em.'

'What you do?'

'Journalist.'

'No shit?'

'No shit.'

'So what you doing now?'

'Just travelling around.'

'Which is why you're here?'

'You got it.'

'Well, you have landed yourself in one crazy fucking place.'

'That a fact?'

'Tell you, Darwin is just the best. Great beaches, great bars, great casinos, and plenty of great babes to pump your "nads".'

The stripper was now on the edge of the stage, grabbing a ten-dollar note from some old guy with three teeth and red rheumy eyes. In exchange for the ten-spot, Grandpa was allowed a quick facial encounter with Madame's nether regions. The problem was, as soon as he went to work, he got hit with a sneezing fit. A very wet sneezing fit which caught the stripper full blast.

'Stupid dickhead,' she screamed and bolted for her dressing-room.

'Where you goin?' Grandpa screamed after her. 'I ain't got my money's worth.'

The crowd ate it up. Especially Jerry Watts.

'Man, I love this town,' he said, turning back to his new buddy.

But I was already halfway out the door.

two

It was hot. Blast furnace hot, 103° at midnight hot. Hitting the street was like diving into a vat of cotton candy: no air, solid goo. I wanted to about-face and dive back into the air-conditioned bar, but I knew that Jerry Watts would corner me again with a can of piss and treat me to more of his retarded observations on life-and-babes. *Got me a cute little Filipina girlfriend name of Mamie.* You would, pal. And after Jerry finished his 'Snatches I Have Known Stories', Grandpa might just be wheeled out for a repeat performance with the next stripper on show.

Fuck the heat. I'm walking.

Darwin at midnight. Drunks in khaki shorts slalomed down the streets. A quartet of aboriginals with bare feet sat on the pavement, passing around a bottle of Bundaberg rum. The occasional *femme de nuit* – all hot-pants and peroxide and chapped lips – awaited her next trick in the shadows of a twelve-buck hotel. And every so often, you'd stumble across some member of the local jailbait sorority who'd drunk eight rum and cokes too many and was now losing her lunch in a trash bin.

Man, I love this town. I hated it. Hated it on sight. I'd pulled in yesterday morning off a thirty-six hour flight from Boston via London and Jakarta. After checking into a cheap motel, I'd asked the desk clerk to point me in the direction of downtown.

'You're in it,' he'd said.

Downtown Darwin was a couple of token skyscrapers, a lot of cheap breezeblock buildings and a main drag that had been turned into a concrete shopping mall. The old town had been blown away during a memorable cyclone on Christmas Day 1974, so everything on show was new, but kind of transient and gimcrack. The bargain-basement school of modern architecture. You squander a day and a half in the air and what's the payoff? Landing in a sub-tropical suburbia with tit-shows. At least at night the mercury divebombed from a midday high of 120° down to the low three-figures. But night in Darwin was when the crazies came out. Night was when the town belonged to Jerry Watts and Grandpa and . . .

'You looking for a party, mate?'

A voice from the dark. I kept walking, but the voice pursued me.

'I *said*, you looking for a party?'

I spun around. Behind me, stepping out of a beat-up Holden, was a rail-thin kid around twenty-one. Long stringy hair, a pack of cigarettes rolled up in his T-shirt sleeve, and eyes as glassy as an ice-cube. They were eyes that made you wonder if the kid's frontal lobe had been tampered with. They were eyes that spelled trouble.

'I ask a question, I expect a bloody answer,' the kid said. 'You want a girl?'

Squeezed into the front passenger seat of the Holden was a woman who weighed around 250lbs. She was readjusting her lipstick in the rearview mirror and puffing on a cigarette at the same time. She had a treble chin and oozed cellulite. Her John could have marketed her with the slogan *Can Sleep Two Comfortably*.

'You want her?' the kid asked again.

'No thanks,' I said.

'I tell you, she's good. She's real good. I *know* she's good. She's my wife.'

I turned tail, picking up speed as the kid yelled after me: 'Fucking Yank wanker . . . fucking Yank shirt-lifter . . .'

The perfect end to a perfect evening in Darwin.

It was only a two-block canter to my motel. I jogged into the forecourt, spun around once to make certain the kid wasn't pursuing me with his freak-show wife, and then made a bee-line for my rented unit. It was adjacent to a swimming pool which featured peeling paint and scummy water. I fumbled with the keys, finally managed to spring the lock, and slammed the door on the night.

The room: a concrete box painted pink, a patterned nylon carpet pockmarked by cigarette burns, a lump-infested bed, a fridge that didn't work, a pay TV, a geriatric air-conditioner. I'd left the machine on while I was out, but the room was still a Turkish bath. So I stripped off my sweat-soaked clothes, kicked the congealed bundle into a corner, and took refuge in the shower. The water was arctic-cold. It was also a little brown, but I wasn't complaining. Anything that drowned the Darwin day was all right by me.

The motel towels were as thin as a communion wafer and about as absorbent. I tried to wrap one around my waist, but was defeated by 20lbs of excess flab. So I improvised, fashioning the towel into a makeshift loincloth tied below the hip. In the process, I caught a snapshot glimpse of myself in the bathroom mirror. I didn't like the picture: a thirty-eight-year-old with all the usual signs of midlife negligence. I had a

soft, burgeoning belly and a nasty crab-apple of fat beneath
my chin. My sandy hair was mottled with grey. There were
permanent dark smudges of fatigue below my eyes and a rail-
road map of lines branching out to my temples. I looked tired,
bloated, world-weary.

A cigarette was needed. Before I'd left the States I'd started
smoking again after a seven-year hiatus. I was now on two
packs of unfiltered Camels a day. My old wheeze had
returned. I was coughing up a brown oyster of phlegm every
morning. My teeth were turning a nice shade of terracotta.
Going back on the smokes was the most positive thing I'd
done in years.

My duty-free carton of Camels was by the bed. I fished
out a fresh pack, tapped out a weed, lit it with my Zippo,
inhaled deeply. Bingo. Instant elation. Why spend a lifetime
chasing happiness when the only no-bullshit bliss you ever
encounter is fleeting, incidental: a shower after a hot day; a
cigarette which tastes so damn good you think you've finally
bumped into serenity. For a moment or two anyway.

My encounter with serenity was a quickie. It ended when I
looked at the map of Australia that I'd left spread out across
the bed. That dumbshit map. I'd been seduced by it.
Seduced by its possibilities. That map had brought me here.
To Darwin. That map had been a serious mistake.

I'd first seen the map in a Boston bookshop. It was a
washed-out afternoon in February, very cold, very grey. A few
days earlier, I'd walked out of a job on a newspaper in Maine.
It was the fourth journalistic gig that I'd abandoned in the past
decade. I'd always worked for provincial newspapers – an itinerant hack-for-hire, roaming the eastern seaboard in a battered
Volvo. I'd done time in Schenectady, New York; in Scranton,
Pennsylvania; in Worcester, Massachusetts; in Augusta,
Maine. A string of smalltime journals in a string of smalltime
cities. Sometimes my colleagues on these papers wondered
why I had this predilection for finding work in battered factory towns; why, after a decade on the journalistic road, I

hadn't tried my luck on some big-time rag in Philly or Boston or even The Apple. But I wasn't interested in exploring the higher reaches of the journalistic firmament. I liked cruising through the middling stratosphere – because there was never any chance of letting ambition bind me to any one spot. Two years of reporting municipal council meetings, church fêtes, and the occasional teenage pile-up on the Interstate, and I was ready to move on. Which is why, after twenty-eight months on the *Augusta Kennebec Journal*, I tendered my notice, packed my worldly possessions into the back of my Volvo station wagon, and headed south on I-95.

I was en route to a new job on the Akron Ohio *Beacon Journal*. But before beginning a two-year stint in the rubber tyre capital of America, I decided to spend a few days drifting through Boston. So I checked into a cheap hotel off Bolyston Street, took the trolley across the Charles to Cambridge, and hit the used bookshops around Harvard Square. I found the map in the first one I walked into. I was browsing through the travel section when I saw a cardboard box crammed with old road maps. Amidst an all-American collection of highway cartography, I stumbled across an anomaly: a 1957 Royal Automobile Club map of Australia. Price: $1.75. I opened it up, spreading it out on the bookshop floor. It was unlike any map I'd ever seen: an island the size of America with only one road crossing its vacant midsection and one road circumnavigating the entire continent.

A shop assistant stumbled upon me kneeling above Australia.

'You gonna buy that map or what?' the shop assistant said.

'Yeah,' I said. 'I'll buy it.'

I didn't simply buy the map, I also stopped by the Harvard Co-op and picked up a guide to Australia. Inside there was a more up-to-date map of the country's thoroughfares – and I was intrigued to discover that there was still only one road bisecting its centre and one hugging its coast. This wasn't a real country, this was some sort of fictive frontier. The Big Nowhere.

13

I returned to my hotel room, ordered up a pizza and a six-pack of Schlitz, and spent the evening dallying in the land of Oz. My eye kept fastening on the city of Darwin. Geographically speaking, it was a real back-of-beyond burgh – the High North midpoint for the road that ringed the continent. Due East was a state called Queensland – famed (according to the guidebook) for its fruit plantations, its tropical swelter, its redneck politics – making me think that it must be twinned with Mississippi. Due West, however, you entered a realm of peculiar enchantment.

Imagine travelling for a thousand miles and never encountering any signs of twentieth-century life, the guidebook said. *Imagine wide-open country under brilliant cobalt-blue skies, far far away from the cares and pressures of modern-day existence. The 3,000-mile road from Darwin to Perth not only brings you through the heart of the natural wonder that is the West Australian Outback, it also gives you access to the last great wilderness on the planet.*

Now I knew that I was being fed a heavy dose of copywriter cant – but I still couldn't take my eyes off that map. All that space; all that *nothing*. Sitting in that cheap hotel room – eating a cold slice of pepperoni pizza which leaked grease on to Darwin and environs – it suddenly struck me that I'd never really been anywhere. All right, I'd spent the last fifteen years rambling around the east coast like some sort of journalistic Flying Dutchman – but, bar a week-long trip to London a couple of years ago, I knew nothing of the world beyond I-95. And now, here I was – a guy on the frontier of the Big Four-O – about to get locked into another two-bit job on another two-bit newspaper. In Akron-fucking-Ohio. Where they made Goodyear radials and little else. Two years there would be like overdosing on embalming fluid. Why embrace the lacklustre option yet again? Especially since I had no ties, no commitments. And if I really was the unencumbered dude I fancied myself to be, then wasn't it time to get off the hack treadmill for a while and disappear into the Great Wide Open?

I ruminated on this question while working my way

through that six-of-Schlitz, a pack of Camels, and a couple of late-night movies on TV. Somewhere between a remake of *Brief Encounter* set in a suburb of Honolulu and a cheap horror flick about giant killer rabbits attacking a National Guard outpost, I blew lunch. An amalgamation of cold pizza, cheap lager, twenty cigarettes and homicidal bunnies pushed my gut over the edge. But while hugging the porcelain, my mind became peculiarly clear. So clear, in fact, that by the time the final cascade of vomit had hit the water, I'd decided that I was en route to the Outback.

And now, sitting in that cheap sweat-box of a room in Darwin, I marvelled at my profound, far-reaching stupidity. I discover an old map in a Boston bookshop and a couple of hours later – while tossing my cookies in some fleabag hotel – I decide to run off to the ass end of Australia. I call my future employers and politely tell them to stuff their job. I put everything I own into storage. I sell my beloved Volvo. I withdraw my life savings of $10,000. I get a visa. I buy a plane ticket. A day and a half later, I land here. The moral of the story: fall in love with a map and you fuck up your life.

Outside the hotel room, the night sky began to put on a show. First came three heavy-metal claps of thunder. Then there was a quick flash of lightning, followed by rain. A power shower of tropical rain. Ten inches in ten seconds. A deluge so frenzied that it knocked out a power cable near the hotel. It left me sitting alone in the dark. As the monsoon crashed around me, I cheered it on, hoping it might just wash Darwin – and all my mistakes – away.

three

As soon as I saw the van, I knew I was going to buy it. It was a classic: a Volkswagen microbus, circa 1970; a true period piece which took me back to my student days — when every counterculture clown bought a cheap van, sprayed it pink and then headed off to commune with the karma of the American road. This VW, on the other hand, looked like it was built to commune with a demilitarized zone, as it had been done up in brown and green camouflage colours. Too bad this wasn't Saigon 1968, 'cause all this baby needed was a machine-gun nest on the roof and it would've been ready to rock-and-roll its way to the Tet Offensive. German engineering meets American depravity. *Guten morgen, Vietnam.*

17

The van was parked opposite my hotel. It was one of a dozen or so camping vehicles lining the street – for this was Darwin's unofficial van market; the place where travel-weary veterans of the Australian road came to sell their wheels to anyone venturing out into the bush. There were standard four-wheel-drive pickups, and trailers hauled by clapped-out Holdens, and even a Bedford van with a lop-sided peace sign daubed on its bonnet. But there was only one VW microbus – and I immediately approached it.

Up close, the camouflage paint-job appeared to be the work of a spastic and one wing was perforated by rust. But the tyres seemed solid and there was a reassuring spring to the chassis when I bounced my foot off the front fender. Peering through the windscreen, however, I found myself face to face with a bare-chested young woman, a tiny infant fastened to one nipple. I turned assorted shades of red, but the woman simply smiled a beatific smile.

Then the rear door of the van slid open and out came this six-foot-four stringbean with shoulder-length hair and a chunky copper crucifix dangling around his neck. He stood motionless by the side of the van, staring at me – a vacant, miles-from-nowhere gaze that made me very nervous.

'Sorry, I tested your suspension like that,' I said. 'Didn't realize you were in there.'

No response from the man who looked like a refugee from Jonestown – just another long vacuous gawk. Finally he spoke:

'Twenty-five hundred dollars.' He took a step towards me. 'Twenty-five hundred dollars,' he said again, bringing his face in so close that I found myself staring up into two thick rain forests of nasal hair. 'That's the price of the van – Two-Five-O-O.'

I took a step backwards. 'What makes you think I want to buy it?'

'You want it. I can tell.'

'Mind if I look it over?'

'No need. It's perfect.'

'A nineteen-year-old vehicle is never perfect.'

'This one's twenty years old. Year of manufacture was One-Nine-Seven-Two. And it *is* perfect.'

'I'm not going to buy it without checking it out mechanically.'

'What you want to know?'

'Mileage on the clock.'

'One-Two-Eight.'

'A hundred and twenty-eight *thousand* miles?'

'That's what I said.'

'The thing must be on its last legs.'

'Got a rebuilt engine, new carburettor, new shocks, new radiator, new cooking stove in the back, new mattress on the bunk bed . . . and it also happens to be blessed.'

'Blessed?'

'Yeah, *blessed*. Been right round the country twice – and it's never suffered one bit of Satanic interference.'

'Satanic interference?'

'Engine break-down, overheating, busted clutch . . .'

'A busted clutch is Satanic interference?'

'Satan always wants to interfere with a messenger of God.'

'Is that your line of work?'

'I preach the Gospel of Jesus Christ, yes.'

'Where's your parish?'

'Out there,' the man said, pointing to the empty world beyond the city limits. 'Five years I've been in the bush, spreading the word.'

'You with some kind of church?'

'My own. The Apostolic Church of Unconditional Faith. You know what *unconditional faith* is, brother?'

'Can't say that I do.'

The man rolled up his right shirt-sleeve, exposing an arm pockmarked by a half-dozen or so bite scars. 'Ever heard of a King Brown snake?' he asked.

19

I shook my head.

'Nastiest viper there is in the bush. They sink their fangs in you, you're dead within an hour. But they've bitten me three times and I'm still here. Know why? Unconditional faith. *They shall take up serpents and if they drink any deadly thing it shall not hurt them* – Mark 16, verse 18. You see what I'm getting at? You see what I'm trying to *share* with you?'

'I think so.'

'Why you buying this van?'

'I didn't say I was buying it . . .'

'You *are* buying it. Now why?'

'Travelling around. Working my way south to Perth, that's all.'

'You know what you're heading into, brother? An evil pagan wasteland which God created to test his flock. And let me give you a piece of spiritual advice – you venture out into those badlands without *unconditional faith* and it'll swallow you up. Swallow you up whole.'

I turned away from this whacked-out snake-handler, glancing briefly at the bush which encircled Darwin. From here, it looked about as threatening as a suburban park: a green-and-pleasant veldt of tropical foliage. Enough of this clown's Old Testament rantings. Let's take a look at what's under the hood.

'Like I told you before,' I said, 'you want to sell the bus, you're going to have to let me check it out. No inspection, no sale.'

A grand canyon of a silence passed while the snake-handler thought this over. Then he tapped on a window and said, 'Bathsheba, come on out of there and bring my tool-kit.'

The rear door slid open again and out came Bathsheba, the tiny infant in one arm, a rusted workbox in the other, and a matching copper crucifix bouncing between her now-covered breasts. She smiled at me again.

'G'day, brother.'

Her husband relieved her of the tool-kit, pointed to a spot on the ground beneath a palm tree and said, 'Sit there.'

With another smile, she did as ordered, cradling the infant in her lap. Then the snake-handler dropped the tool-kit at my feet.

'Go to work,' he said.

I actually know a thing or two about internal combustion, having once taken a DIY course in car repair when I was deeply infatuated with my late lamented Volvo. So for the next two hours, I performed a mechanical autopsy on the microbus – poking my way into valves, exploring the mysteries of the crank shaft, making certain that the carburettor, the alternator and the distributor could face another lengthy jaunt into the bush. It was monotonous, grimy work, not aided by the high intensity arrival of the late-morning sun. But the heat wasn't half as annoying as the sight of Mr Unconditional Faith and his wife sitting under a palm tree, silently watching me dissect their vehicle. They were so motionless, so goddamn still, that I figured they must've checked into some sort of spiritual Twilight Zone. It was deeply disconcerting to have a pair of zombies fix you in their gaze for two solid hours, but it did encourage me to work fast so I could get the job done, hand over the requisite cash, and say a permanent goodbye to this pair of space cadets. Happily, the van was in operative shape. There was a reassuring hum to the engine, it had new plugs and points, the timing seemed spot-on, and all other mechanical parts appeared to be doing their job properly. Even the tiny living area at the rear – two narrow bunkbeds, a hot-plate, and a tiny fridge that was powered by a battery – was tolerably clean. As long as I looked after it on the road, I figured that I should get close to what I paid for it when I finally reached Perth.

Yeah. This'll do.

'Okay, Reverend,' I said, closing the hood with a definitive thud. 'Let's do business.'

'Two-Five-O-O is the price. Two-Five-O-O is what you're gonna pay.'

'No one ever pays the asking price for a car.'

'You want the van, you pay what I ask.'

'Forget it.'

'Right, then. Bathsheba, we'll be leaving now.'

They stood up and returned to the van. I couldn't believe it – the asshole really was going to drive away.

'Come on, come on,' I shouted after them. 'Can't we do a deal?'

'Messengers of God make no deals.' With that, the snake-handler started up the engine, released the emergency brake and slowly cruised off down the road. Idiot that I am, I gave pursuit – running alongside the microbus, pounding on its side and yelling, 'All right, all right, I'll pay your goddamn price.'

Three hours later – after cashing a small wad of traveller's cheques, visiting an insurance broker, and making the requisite pilgrimage to the local car registry bureau – I owned the microbus. When I returned to the van, I found the snake-handler sitting with his wife and infant son in the same patch of shade. The back of the bus had been scrubbed clean and their worldly possessions were stuffed into two small duffel bags leaning against a side door. As my gut did cartwheels, I handed over twenty-five $100-notes. The snake-handler counted and recounted the dough before finally presenting me with the keys. They were attached to a crucifix keyring.

'What's next for you guys?' I asked.

'Missionary work in Darwin,' the snake-handler said. 'This city needs us.'

'You'll do well here. Real well. Especially the snake stuff. That should go down a treat.'

'His will be done.'

'One last thing,' I said. 'Was it you who painted the van camouflage?'

'Yes, it was us.'

'Mind me asking *why?*'
'So Satan wouldn't see us coming, that's why.'
With that, the entire adult membership of The Apostolic
Church of Unconditional Faith hoisted a bag each and wandered off into the midday sun.

four

Two hours out of Darwin, I hit my first kangaroo. It was night – the darkest night I had ever ventured into. Growing up in rural Maine, I was accustomed to negotiating open country after sundown. But this was different. No moonlight, no roadlamps, no competing highbeams from other cars, not even the hint of a constellation in the overcast sky. Just absolute blackness. Yet every mile or so, the headlights of the microbus would pick out two radiant embers in the near-distance – tiny beaming eyeballs which seemed to be floating in that opaque void. They made me grip the wheel a little tighter – because something out there was watching me.

Then, suddenly, there was this nasty thud. It sent me flying into the steering wheel as the front of the van slammed into some invisible hulk. It also managed to jam the car horn.

Adrenalin-drunk with shock, I scrambled out of the cab. Bad idea. As my right foot touched the road, it made direct contact with the cause of the accident – the now-inanimate body of an five-foot kangaroo. I tried to jump away from the carcass, but I slipped, my sneakers skating across the pool of blood which engulfed the dead animal. I landed ass-first on the road. Now, alongside a bruised set of ribs, I could add a contused coccyx to my list of injuries. Getting up was a struggle – but the pain involved in scrambling to my feet was preferable to lying next to a broken-necked beast with blood still pumping from its nostrils. I staggered to the cab, dug out my flashlight and inspected the damage: a cracked lens on one of the lights, a sizeable dent along the front bumper and little else. As kangaroo accidents go, I'd had a lucky call. I must have winged the 'roo in mid-bounce, throwing it clear of the vehicle. Had I hit it head-on, the microbus would now look like a German-built accordion. But even though I'd gotten off lightly, I was still furious. Furious with myself for breaking a major rule of the Outback: *never hit the road after dark*. Every guidebook I'd read had warned me of the potential dangers involved in night-time navigation and emphasized that itinerant 'roos were a real hazard come sundown. But in my moronic rush to get out of Darwin, I'd forgotten such counsel, and also hadn't given myself any time to adjust to driving on the wrong side of the road. Instead, I'd headed south immediately – clearing out my motel room, shopping for provisions, and roaring out of town within an hour of taking possession of the van. Yet another inane act of impulsiveness. Yet another major fuck-up.

The still-blaring car horn was not helping my mood, so I grabbed the tool-kit, popped the bonnet and went digging around assorted cables before I spotted the source of the commotion: a bit of gouged metal pressing on the cord for the horn. Quick radical surgery was demanded – and, to free up my hands for the job, I gripped the torch between my teeth, then snapped the cord with a pair of pliers.

Silence. Deep cavernous silence. The sort of silence which

can lead you to believe that you are all alone in the world. It made me jittery, this limitless hush. Because it made me realize that I had crossed the frontier into Nowheresville.

I scrambled back into the cab and pulled the van off the road. After killing the engine, I climbed into the living area, lit the oil lamp I'd bought before leaving Darwin, struck another match to a cigarette, drew the smoke deep into my lungs, and suddenly felt as if some heavyweight had caught me with a right to the chest. The pain was spectacular. Stripping off my shirt, I stared down at two blotchy bruises adorning my thorax. They reminded me of a Rorschach Test. What do these ink-blots call to mind, Mr Hawthorne? Some clown in a van hitting a kangaroo.

There was no tape in the first-aid kit, no ice in the tiny freezer compartment at the top of the fridge. So I grabbed two cold cans of Swan Export, applied one to my chest and downed the other in a very long slurp. Then I fished out a box of aspirin, popped three pills in my gullet and chased them with another beer. A third can of Swan and the pain began to deaden. A fourth and the pain had moved off to another town. A fifth and I was down for the count on the bunk-bed.

I woke just before daybreak. The lager-and-aspirin anaesthetic had worn off and I was hurting. The pain was now quadrophonic, blaring out from my left- and right-ribcage, my tailbone, my morning-after head. I lay on my bunk-bed, a vision of pure misery. This is the shittiest morning of my life. I want to die. Now.

The urge for a quick death was superseded by an even greater urge to pee. I spent the requisite ten minutes debating whether getting up was a more painful prospect than remaining prone in bed with an excruciatingly full bladder. My bladder won the argument. A countdown, please. Five, four, three, two, one . . . The back door of the van crashed open and a long, hard stream of urine baptized the Outback clay.

It was no fun being up on my feet, trying to unstiffen my arthritic body. It was no fun catching sight of the dead kangaroo, its glazed eyes staring at me with mournful reproach. Overhead, a pair of buzzards were on a reconnaissance flight, checking out the prospects of a kangaroo breakfast. I watched these winged mercenaries in near-darkness – the heavens an opaque canvas with only one small pinhole of light on the distant horizon. But soon the pinhole enlarged and lengthened and grew molten. Night woke up, the blackened sky parting at the middle to reveal the ferocity of the early morning sun.

As this harsh sphere began to gain altitude, I blinked madly in its glare. Once my eyes adjusted to the light, I saw where I was . . . and I was transfixed.

I was in a world rendered red. An arid red, like the colour of dried blood. A non-stop vista of red clay and red scrubby bush. It stretched across a plateau of incalculable dimensions. I walked away from the van, stood in the middle of the road and turned north, south, east, west. No houses, no telephone poles, no billboards, no roadsigns . . . no hints whatsoever (bar the strip of tarmacadam I was standing on) that man had ever been acquainted with this territory. Just hard barren country under a hard blue sky. Measureless in its dimensions, hypnotic in its monotony.

What century am I in? Check that: what geologic era? We're talking Palaeozoic, I think. We're talking Genesis 1:1.

Stepping off the road, I took a few tentative steps into the bush. It was like sticking an exploratory toe into a vast ocean that could easily swallow me whole. The baked sand crackled underfoot as I ventured in for a few yards, edging my way through a thicket of Spinifex – a desert plant which looked a bit like an anorexic cactus. Spinifex blanketed the landscape, its parched flora accentuating the terrain's wasteland status. I hiked on, my eyes firmly fixed on the indeterminate horizon. I could keep on walking for the next twelve hours and, by sunset, I'm sure I would still be in the same big patch of bush – because I am now standing in the geographic equivalent of infinity.

I could keep on walking for the next twelve hours and, by sunset, I'm sure I would also be dead of thirst.

That was a spooky thought – the realization that, if I continued to amble on, the final destination would be the end of my life. It made me about-face and head back to the safety of the van. The sun was now turning on the wattage, my throat was Mojave-dry from my hangover, and the shirt and jeans I had slept in were beginning to fuse to my still-stiff body. By the time I reached the vehicle I needed a further dose of anaesthetics to keep the pain at bay, so breakfast was three aspirin and two more cans of Swan lager. Then it was time for a bath. I pulled off my clothes, filled a plastic bucket with rusty water from a jerry-can, and dumped the lot over my skull. End of bath.

I changed into a pair of shorts and a T-shirt, slid behind the wheel, readjusted the seat-belt so that it didn't press too hard on my bruised ribcage, and prepared to drive off. Before I did, though, I stared back out at that expanse of bush into which I'd briefly tramped. This is what I came to see. A prehistoric landscape – formidable, fearful. The beginning of the world . . . or the end of it. A void to match my own.

But now that I'd seen it – now that I'd been shown irrefutable visual proof of my total insignificance – I need see no more. The Outback? Been there, done that.

For a few heady moments, I toyed with a fantasy: I'd drive straight back to Darwin, get on the blower to the Akron Ohio *Beacon Journal* and talk myself back into the job I'd turned down. Then I'd re-sell the van to some other crazy schmuck heeding the call of the wild and grab the first plane headed Stateside. It was a cut-your-losses fantasy – a scenario which (if I acted it out) would confirm everything I always feared about myself: my inability to see any project or plan through to the end, my entrenched parochialism, my distrust of the world beyond my narrow little domain of experience. For a quarter of an hour, I sat there, the engine idling, trying to convince myself that I could live with this self-knowledge. I had two geographic options: north to the mundane, south to the unknown. I wanted north, but put the van into gear and continued drifting south.

As I pulled away, I glanced in my rearview mirror just as the two buzzards swooped down on the kangaroo, each plucking out an eye before soaring off. I didn't look back again.

I drove for hours and saw nothing. Nothing but the same boundless sweep of bush. By noon, I'd chewed up 400k of geography, but hadn't encountered another vehicle. The heat was now insane, so I sought relief from the fan in my van. A big mistake: instead of circulating cool air around the cab, it belched red road dust which covered me in grit. I wanted to pull over, pop the bonnet and figure out why all that dust was breaching the ventilation system, but I sensed that carrying out repairs under that brutish sun might prove dangerous to my health. So I continued to push on, the grit on my body turning into sweat-induced mud.

Around a hundred kilometres later – just when my brain was beginning to feel drycleaned by dehydration – I saw something very welcome in the distance: a gas station. It was the first gas station I'd encountered since leaving Darwin. It wasn't much of an establishment: a grim jerry-built bunker with two pumps out front. But after a night and a morning of extreme Outback solitude, the sight of any man-made object – even a concrete latrine – would have hoisted my morale.

The proprietor stood in the doorway. He was built like the bunker he inhabited: short and squat, with permanent five o'clock shadow and a T-shirt that appeared to have been used as a handkerchief.

'G'day,' he said in a toneless voice.

'Howdy,' I said. 'You got a shower here I might be able to use?'

'Cost you ten dollars.'

'Ten bucks for a shower?'

'That's what I said.'

'That's a crazy price.'

'You feel that way, you can wait until Kununurra.'

'What's Kununurra?'

'The next town . . . and the next place you'll find a shower.'

'How far away?'

''Round six hundred kilometres.'

'You're shitting me?'

'Start driving and see for yourself.'

The thought of five more grit-caked hours on that hot open road was not a nice one. I forked over the ten bucks.

'Shower's out back next to the pisser,' the proprietor said. 'Want me to fill it up?'

'Yeah . . . and check the water and oil while you're at it.'

The proprietor sidled over to the van, his eyes taking in the smashed front light, the dented front bumper.

'You hit a 'roo?' he said.

The shower was an open stall situated next to a trough that served as a urinal. Ten years of cigarette butts plugged the drain. The stench was so staggering I had to hold my breath as I stood under the showerhead. The water pressure was good, though. Too good. It reactivated the pain around my bruised ribs and forced me out of the shower sooner than I wished. I pulled on my shorts and runners and walked back to the van dripping wet. Sitting in the passenger seat of my cab was an elderly aboriginal man. He appeared to have dozed off, his bare, dusty feet resting on the dashboard.

'Hey, what's that guy doing in my van?'

The proprietor stuck his head out from under the bonnet and sized up the black-and-blue splotches on my chest.

'You really did hit a 'roo, didn't you?'

'I said, what the hell is that guy doing asleep in my van?'

'That's Titus. He's from around here, and he needs a lift south.'

Titus opened one eye in greeting, then shut it and dozed off again.

'Well, thanks for asking me.'

The proprietor slammed the bonnet shut and wiped his oil-slicked hands on his T-shirt.

'Your 'roo did a little damage to your ventilating system,' he said.

'Tell me about it,' I said. 'You wouldn't happen to have a spare radiator grille handy?'

'Kununurra's where you'll find spares. Kununurra's where you'll find everything up here.'

'Six hundred kilometres, you said?'

'Yeah, six hundred kilometres. You should just about make it by dark . . . if you don't bump into another 'roo.'

'What do I owe you for the juice?'

'Forty-two dollars.'

'Don't shit me again.'

'Look at the pump, you don't believe me.'

'Forty-two bucks for a tank of gas? That's idiotic.'

'No, mate. That's *the price*.'

I paid the slob off and drove away. Titus remained comatose in the front seat: a man around sixty-five with a face more creviced than a bas-relief.

'So where you going?' I finally asked him.

Another feline squint from Titus. 'Down the road.'

'How far down the road?'

'I'll let you know when I want you to stop.'

'Much appreciated.'

'You're East Coast, aren't you?'

'Sorry?'

'You're from New England. Maine, perhaps?'

I stared at Titus, astounded. 'You've been over there?'

'Never been out of the Northern Territory.'

'Then how did you know my accent?'

'I listen to voices, that's all.'

He shut his eyes again and nodded off, killing off any further conversational possibilities. Around fifteen minutes later, he shook himself awake and said, 'I'll jump here.'

But we were still deep in the bush, with not a village or

dwelling in sight.

'You want to get out *here*?' I said, bringing the van to a stop. Titus nodded.

'But where are you headed?'

Titus cocked a thumb towards the open plateau. 'Out there,' he said.

'But what's there?'

'Nothing you want to see.' He opened the door and climbed down into the red dirt. 'Piece of advice, mate. Don't go out there. Keep on the main road.'

'What d'you mean by that?'

'I mean *nothing*. I'm just telling you: stay away from any unpaved tracks. Stick to the bitumen.'

'Why?'

'Because you're a main road man, that's why.'

He turned and started walking into the bush. I watched him saunter off, envious. Envious that someone could be so comfortable within this vacuum.

'*You're a main road man.*' Got me in one, asshole.

And for the next five hours, I hugged that road until it brought me back to something approximating civilization.

five

In the town of Kununurra, I found a radiator grille for my van. And surgical tape for my bruised ribs. And a municipal shower which only cost a buck a blast.

I took three showers a day, flushing away the dusty stench of the Outback. Keeping clean became an obsession – a way of maintaining some discipline in an undisciplined place. Especially since Kununurra was a burgh which encouraged you to turn seedy. It was a prefabricated collection of shops and greasy spoons and bars: a scruffy little gasoline alley in the middle of the bush. You weren't supposed to linger for long in Kununurra – it was a pit-stop, a place to stock up on supplies and human contact before disappearing off again into empty quarters. But I remained there for nearly a week, parking my van at an in-town campsite. Initially, I convinced myself that I needed some time to recuperate from my kangaroo encounter. After four days, however, my ribcage had lost its inky colour and my coccyx no longer felt pulverized. 'I'll just hang on for another day,' I told myself, trying to forestall my departure back into the bush. When that day passed, I decided that it would take another forty-eight hours for my 'roo wounds to be completely healed. So I continued to convalesce in the back of the van, reading a pile of cheap thrillers I bought in a local thrift shop, only venturing out to pick up tinned provisions and make my thrice-daily pilgrimage to the public baths.

Six days after my arrival in Kununurra, a campsite official dropped by the van and gave me a verbal eviction notice.

'You're here a week tomorrow,' she said. 'And seven days is the maximum anyone can stay, so you've got to push off.'

The official was a tired woman in her fifties, a cigarette welded to her lips, her skin the texture of rawhide. I wondered if she was bribeable.

'Any chance you could bend the rules a bit?' I asked.

'No way, mate.'

'Listen, I'm resting up after an accident.'

'You don't look injured to me.'

'Check out the front of the van, if you don't believe me.'

She gave it a cursory glance. Though the radiator grille had been replaced, the bumper was still badly dented.

'A 'roo, right?'

'Yeah.'

'Bet you were driving at night.'

I stared at my shoes.

'Only fuckwits drive at night up here. And fuckwits get no sympathy from me.'

I held up a twenty-dollar note.

'You must be joking.'

I held up a second twenty-dollar note. She snatched the cash out of my hand.

'That buys you three more nights starting tomorrow. Then you go.'

'Have a nice day,' I said and closed the van door on her face. Nazi bush bitch . . . Camp counsellor from hell . . .

Then the unease hit. An unease that maybe she was on to something; that maybe I was dawdling too long in Kununurra. Especially since it was a town which held no real attraction for me – bar the fact that it was *a town*. And after that first unnerving foray into the bush, I needed the security of a town. A place where there was plenty of visceral distraction, where you weren't turned in on yourself by all that wide open space. That was the real danger of the Outback: the way its emptiness heightened your creeping self-doubt. Forget all that crap you hear about scenic grandeur making all your insecurities appear insignificant. If anything, it amplifies every little fear, every tendency towards self-loathing. Because this terrain informs you: *you are nothing*. Better to cling to a town, where there's safety in numbers.

Where you don't have to be alone with yourself.

But while I was reluctant to leave town, I was distinctly troubled about loitering in Kununurra without much intent. I couldn't exactly pinpoint the cause of this free-floating apprehension. It was simply an odd feeling that I was overstaying my welcome. Hit the road, Jack – before you take root here. All right, all right – but give me three more bush-free days.

Three more days, nine more showers. On the morning of the fourth day, I walked over to the municipal baths for one final dousing, standing under the spray for the better part of a half-hour, reluctant to leave its cool comfort. When I got back to the van, the campsite official was leaning against the cab, flicking cigarette ash on the bonnet.

'I told you I wanted you out of here this morning,' she said.

I brushed by her and climbed into the driving seat.

'I'm gone,' I said, cranking up the engine.

'Where you heading?' she asked.

'Far away from you,' I said and roared off.

The fact was, though – I really didn't know where I was going. The next large town down the road was called

Broome – a mere 1,000k away. In between, there was a pair of inconsequential hamlets and a lot of open country. If I drove non-stop for the next eight hours, I might just make the first of those habitable dots on the map by sundown. And then? I'll deal with that little dilemma tomorrow. Just get me to the next community before dark and I'll be happy.

I stopped at a gas station on the outer limits of Kununurra. I really didn't need to stop there, as I'd filled up the van yesterday. But when I saw a sign posted before its entrance – LAST PETROL FOR 400K – I got anxious. Even though I knew that the VW would do nearly 500k on a full tank, I still had paranoid visions of being stranded without fuel in some corner of the wild. Best to play Mr Caution and top up the spare jerry-can.

The truck stop was self-service – and after pumping gas, I buried myself beneath the hood. Granted, I realized that there was something a little anal about checking every mechanical corner of the engine, but I was taking no chances before plunging back into the bush.

Around ten minutes into this inspection, I looked up for a moment and caught sight of a young woman, sitting by the side of the road opposite the station, staring at me with peculiar intensity. She was in her early twenties, ample, big-boned, with short sandy blonde hair and a been-there-since-birth suntan. Her clothes were a throwback to the sixties: a tie-dyed T-shirt, cut-off denims, a pair of beach thongs and an old army rucksack with a peace sign stitched across its front. Woodstock Here We Come – only she was probably born a good five years after Woodstock.

'Hiya,' she shouted after catching my eye. 'You going east?'

'Yeah . . . but if you're sitting on that side of the road, aren't you heading into town?'

'Not anymore.'

She stood up and crossed the road towards me. I now noticed that she really was a surfin' girl Valkyrie: around six feet tall, solid muscle, paw-like hands that probably knew a thing or two about manual labour. Not the sort of woman you'd want to pick a fight with – but attractive in a rough-and-tumble way.

'Name's Angie,' she said, crunching my fingers in a chiropractic handshake.

'Nick,' I said, disengaging myself from her grip.

'You a Yank, Nick?'

'I am.'

'Never met a Yank before.'

'You're joking?'

'Don't get too many Yanks where I'm from.'

'Where's that?'

'Little village called Wollanup.'

'Never heard of it.'

'Around fourteen hundred clicks due southwest of here. Smack dab in the Dead Heart.'

'The Dead Heart?'

'Centre of Australia. Y'know, Woop-Woop.'

'Woop-Woop?'

'Bloody wilderness, mate. Bloody back-of-beyond. Where nobody lives.'

'Except you.'

'Never lived anywhere else. Never wanted to, 'cause Wollanup's beaut. Old desert mining town. Only fifty-three of us there and over fourteen hundred clicks to the next village.'

'Sounds great.'

'It is.'

'You coming from there?'

'Kinda. Been on the road for a couple weeks. Just travelling around for a bit.'

'Me too.'

'Where you going now?'

'Direction of Broome, I guess.'

'Then that's where I'm heading.'

She opened the back of the VW and tossed her rucksack inside.

'Your van is a ripper. You in the army?'

'No.'

'Then what's with the paint job?'

'Don't blame me – people I bought it from chose the colours.'

'They must have shit for brains.'

I smiled. 'Got 'em in one.'

'Broome, then?' Angie said.

'Why the change of direction?'

She gave me a jokey punch in the shoulder. ''Cause you're heading that way.'

She opened the passenger door and climbed in. I thought: if this is a pick-up, give this woman a Gold Medal for velocity. And if it's not . . . well, at least I won't be alone in the bush.

'Okay,' I said, sliding behind the wheel. 'Broome.'

We drove off.

'Hey, Nick,' Angie said around a half-mile down the road. 'You're not a God-squadder, are you?'

'No way.'

'Then what's with dippy keyring?'

'You mean the crucifix? It came with the van.'

'Right.' She reached into her pocket and brought out a packet of tobacco and rolling papers. 'Don't like Jesus freaks,' she said, fashioning a cigarette between her fingers.

'You know many?'

'Never met one in my life. Don't have any in Wollanup.'

'Every town has at least one or two holy-rollers.'

'Not Wollanup. No churches, y'see.'

'How'd you manage that?'

'Banned 'em.'

'Isn't that against the law?'

She fished out a wooden match from her tobacco pouch, struck it against her fingernail and lit her cigarette. 'Australian laws ain't Wollanup laws. Smoke?'

Without waiting for an answer, she plugged the roll-up into my mouth. It was my first cigarette since the accident – and though my lungs could now handle the smoke, the initial jolt of nicotine woozied my brain. By the time the second jolt kicked in, I was hooked again.

'You always roll your own?' I asked.

'Never smoked 'em any other way.'

I reached into the glove compartment, dug out a packet of cigarettes and tossed it into her lap, saying, 'Try one of these.'

She studied the packet carefully, running her index finger along its edges as if it were an exotic object. 'Camels?' she said, reading the lettering. 'They any good?'

'Don't tell me you've never had one.'

'Like I said, only ever smoked roll-ups. You can't get anything else in Wollanup.'

'They don't sell *real* cigarettes in your hometown?'

'There's only one shop – and the bloke who owns it likes to roll his own, so that's all he's ever stocked.'

'You mean you've never *seen* a Camel, a Marlboro, a Lucky . . .?'

'Mate, I've never been out of Wollanup.'

'Get outta here . . .'

'Speaking the truth. First time in the big bad world.'

'Twenty-two, twenty-three years in the same town . . .?'

'Twenty-one. I've just turned twenty-one . . .'

' . . . all right, *twenty-one* years in the same nowhere town and you're telling me you never left it *once*?'

She struck another match against her thumbnail, touched it to the tip of the Camel, inhaled deeply. 'When you live in Wollanup, you don't need the rest of the world. You got everything you want right there.' She blew out a small cloud of smoke. 'Not bad . . . for a Yank ciggie.' She flashed me a big smile, her mouth a jumble of stained teeth.

'So if you've never left home before,' I said, 'what made you decide to leave it now?'

'It's kind of a tradition in Wollanup to hit the road when you turn twenty-one, see a bit of the country.'

'Does anyone ever go back?'

'Oh, yeah, everyone. I mean, if you're from Wollanup you're real loyal to the town.'

'All your family there?'

'Yeah, all nine of us.'

'*Nine?*'

'Nine kids, that is . . . plus my two parents . . . so it's really eleven altogether.'

'You mean, a fifth of the population of Wollanup is *your* family?'

'Yeah . . . and the other three families in town make up the rest.'

I had to work hard at suppressing a smirk. Talk about a hick from the sticks. This babe was a true original: Miss Shotgun Shack. From a town with four families, no churches, no factory-made cigarettes and – judging from the state of her teeth – no dentists to boot. Suddenly all those rednecks I'd grown up with in central Maine seemed downright worldly . . . though none of them had her no-bullshit brio, her punchy charm. And snatching a glance at her hefty haunches, I found myself engaged in an enlightened male reverie, the gist of which was: she'd be fun for a night or two.

'How many in your family, Nick?'

'I'm it.'

'Everyone dead?'

'My folks are. Didn't have brothers or sisters.'

'You're an only child?'

'If you don't have siblings, you're generally an only child.'

'No other uncles or cousins anywhere?'

'An old aunt down in Florida, I think . . . but we lost touch after my Mom died five years ago.'

'No one else?'

'That's it.'

'Cripes . . . that really must be weird.'

'What?'

'Knowing that, if you died or disappeared tomorrow, no one would care.'

'Never really think about it.'

'A loner, eh?'

'Guess so.'

'That's kinda sad.'

I could see where this line of questioning was going and I didn't want to get there – because I'd been down this inter-rogatory road before with just about every woman I'd ended up sleeping with. Though I knew that the Little Boy Lost routine was an effective seduction technique, it also meant talking at length about my parents: a subject I preferred to sidestep. Not that they'd been ogres: just a pair of timid elderly depressives who'd accidentally conceived me in their mid-forties and always seemed bemused by my presence. Mr and Mrs Quiet Desperation, whose cosmos never extended beyond the boundaries of the grim mill town where they spent all their lives. The kind of frugal folk who – worried about spending three bucks on a new pair of socks, who even after they paid off their mortgage – remained convinced that their house was going to be repossessed. I'd fled this cheer-less nest at the age of eighteen and only ventured back for a few days at Christmas every year, until old age finally killed them off within six months of each other in 1987. And I never talked about them after that – unless, of course, some woman I was trying to bed started asking me about my 'tragic' lack of family. At which point, I always dodged the issue with some Bogart-esque line like: 'Never lost sleep over it.'

Angie, however, tried to press me further. 'You mean, you really like being alone in the world?'

'I'm used to it, that's all.'

'Wouldn't you like to belong to a family, a community?'

I lied, reasoning that an absolute 'No' might scupper my chances of getting laid before reaching Broome. Better to say something non-committal like: 'Never had the chance really.'

Angie gave me a compassionate, you've-got-a-friend smile and squeezed my arm. 'Maybe you will one day.'

I returned the smile, thinking: the Little Boy Lost routine always does the trick.

We clocked 400k by sundown, gobbling up the mileage with non-stop chat. Angie quizzed me endlessly about the States, wanting to know all about fast food joints and six-lane highways and thirty-six channel television. I found such ingenuousness appealing, though her lack of knowledge about the world beyond Wollanup was breathtaking. Never heard of McDonald's? CNN? Michael Jackson? Lucky you.

Then there were the songs she kept singing to herself: old sixties hits like 'Happy Together' and 'Along Came Mary' and – I couldn't believe it – 'The Ballad of the Green Berets':

> *Back at home a young wife waits*
> *Her Green Beret has met his fate*
> *He has died for those oppressed*
> *Leaving her his last request:*
> *Put silver wings on my son's chest*
> *Make him one of America's best . . .*

I hadn't heard that nuke-the-gooks clunker in around twenty-five years, and wondered why on earth Angie would know the lyrics to a jingoistic classic from the 'Nam years. Angie explained that – since you couldn't get any commercial radio stations in Wollanup (its isolation putting it way out of transmission range) – her musical education was based on a pile of old 45s belonging to one of her uncles (the same guy who gave her the knapsack with the peace sign). And he hadn't bought an album since he moved back to Wollanup in 1972.

'Good Vibrations' . . . 'Downtown' . . . 'We Gotta Get Outta This Place'. Travelling with Angie was like tuning into a Goldie Oldies station – only the disc jockey in charge was a little behind the times when it came to pop music news.

'What's Jim Croce's new record?'

'He's dead.'

'That's the title?'

She was stunned when I explained that the man who'd bequeathed 'Time in a Bottle' to the world had left this life after a plane crash in the seventies. Just as she was also amazed to hear that The Archies had checked into oblivion after releasing 'Sugar, Sugar'. But, yes, Neil Diamond was still going strong, though now his biggest fans were depressed middle-aged women with a penchant for stuffed furry animals.

Angie sang an off-key rendition of 'Sweet Caroline' as we pulled into the hamlet of Hall's Creek, the first of the habitable dots on the map. It was a blink-once-you-miss-it town: a main drag, a couple of side-streets, a post office, a supermarket and a pub, where we sat at the bar and ate incinerated steak with pulpy french fries. We washed down this savourless grub with a six-pack of Export, and Angie put on a show of impressive beer-swilling bravado by downing four of the cans in rapid succession, then throwing ten bucks on the counter and calling for six more coldies.

'You really know how to drink,' I said.

'You live in Wollanup, you know how to drink.'

As Angie popped open another can, a guy around twenty sidled up next to her: an all-denim dude with a leather Stetson crowning his head. He was drunk and flashed her a drunk's hundred-watt grin while helping himself to one of her beers.

'Gidday, Miss Gorgeous Ass.'

'Put it back.'

He flipped open the top and took a long slurp, excess foam running down the side of his face. 'What'd you say, gorgeous ass?'

'I said: put the tinny back.'

Another sloppy slurp from the can of Export. 'Little late now for that, ain't it?'

She gave him an arctic stare. 'You really are a dickhead.'

'So what's that wally you're with gonna do about it?'

Angie immediately stepped off the bar stool and put her face in the face of Mr Denim. 'He's gonna do nothing,' she said, 'because this is between you and me.'

'That a fact, cunt-for-brains.'

She remained very calm, very quiet. And said, 'Take that back.'

'Fuck you.'

'No, mate. Fuck you.' With one rapid motion, her right hand shot out and grabbed Mr Denim's crotch, squeezing his testicles as if they were an exercise ball. And she continued wringing them as she quietly said, 'Apologize.'

Of course, the guy was in no position to apologize, as he was turning blue and bawling for mercy. There must have been a dozen or so hard types at the bar – but no one said a word or tried to break it up. They all just winced. When Angie realized that verbal repentance would not be forthcoming, she shoved him away. He hit the deck and began to emit the sort of howl usually associated with wounded wildlife. Angie grabbed the last of the six-pack in one hand, me in the other, and said, 'Time to go, Yank.'

We walked coolly to the door. But once we hit the street, we broke into a canter, racing to the van. I gunned the engine and we tore off into the night, saying nothing until we were a few miles out of Hall's Creek. Once we were safe within the black vacuum of the bush, Angie told me to pull over and kill the lights. Then – sitting there in the dark – she let out a manic shriek of laughter, cracked open another can of beer and baptized her head with beer.

'Fan-fucking-tastic,' she yelled. 'Death to all dickheads.'

Now it was my turn to be baptized, as Angie shook up the can and sprayed it in my face. I went along with the gag, laughing nervously, yet all the while thinking: this woman is straight out of the Wild West.

'Remind me never to pick a fight with you,' I said.

'Not a chance, mate. Not a chance.'

She made her move, lunging on top of me, grabbing the back of my head and covering my mouth with a deep, vice-like kiss. Before I knew it, I was being pushed out of the driver's seat and on to the rear floor of the van. Then, pinning my arms down with her knees, she tore my T-shirt up the middle and began a suction assault on my chest with her lips. It was like being seduced by a professional wrestler, but I was too dazed to do anything but lie back and be plundered.

Like most assaults, this one was brutal and short. When all the shouting was over, she slumped against my head. Then she took my face in her hands and looked at me long and hard.

'Yeah,' she finally said. 'You'll do.'

six

By the time we were halfway to Broome the following afternoon, I was a very nervous man. There was a basic reason for my disquiet: Angie's ferocious ardour. It was unremitting and bottomless. Her initial Graeco-Roman grapple with me in the back of the van had been a mere appetizer in a carnal pig-out. Having collapsed into sleep after the first onslaught, I was roused two hours later for a second blitzkrieg. Just before dawn, she nudged me back into consciousness with a demand for some oral action. Her idea of a wake-up call also scored points for originality, as I stirred to find her straddling me naked, trying to stimulate my member with one hand while shouting in my ear, 'C'mon, rise and shine.' And when she endeavoured to go down on me around twenty miles along the road to Broome (while I was changing gear, for christsakes), I decided that my prostate could take no more.

'Give it a rest, Angie,' I said, gently attempting to move her face out of my crotch.

'C'mon, it's fun.'

'I'm doing sixty, it's dangerous.'

'Then pull over.'

'Haven't you had enough for one morning?'

'No way.'

'Well, I can't take any more.'

'Got myself an old bull, huh?'

'A *spent* old bull.'

'Looks like I'm gonna have to get you back into shape, lover.'

Lover? Me?

Having managed to negotiate a détente of her sexual bombardment, I still had to put up with three hours of puppy lust. All the way to Broome she kept an arm locked around my neck and constantly nibbled on my ear-lobe. I wondered if she knew the lyrics to 'Teenager in Love'.

I finally said, 'Do you always have this fixation with ears?'

'Nah, yours are the first.'

'What's so special about mine?'

'Nothing really – they're just the first I've nibbled.'

'Your old boyfriends never let you play Bugs Bunny on their ear-lobes?'

'Never had a boyfriend.'

'Bullshit.'

'No bullshit. I mean, how could I, living in Wollanup where everybody's family? Would've been sicko, doing it with a first cousin . . . or one of my brothers.'

I suddenly felt a little queasy.

'You mean . . .'

She gave me this little girl smile and wrapped her arm tighter around my neck. 'That's right, big boy. You were Numero Uno.'

Oh fuck, oh fuck, oh fuck, oh fuck.

I gripped the wheel, stared out at the deep red earth and said nothing. But inside my brain an air raid siren had gone off, warning me of imminent ballistic danger. To an emotional high-roller, unprotected sex with an insatiable virgin probably scored a ten on the testosterone meter. But for someone like me – who has always shunned potentially inflammable situations – it was the equivalent of a kamikaze mission. And one which I was going to bail out of as soon as we made it to Broome.

'You angry or something?' Angie finally said.

'You should have told me . . .'

'Told you what?'

'Told me that I was Number One.'

'You cannot be serious, mate.'

'I am. Very serious.'

'What difference would it have made?'

'It's something a guy should know, that's all.'

'Y'mean, you wouldn't have poked me if you'd known . . . ?'

'I'm not saying that.'

'Then what *are* you saying?'

'Are you on the pill?'

'Shouldn't you have asked me that question last night?'

'Well, are you?'

'Nah.'

I gripped the wheel a little tighter. She gave my left shoulder another of her bruising, playful punches.

'Come on, Nick-boy. No need to go berko on me. Especially since you got nothing to sweat about. My period's due in five days. So there's no danger. No worries.'

'Honest?'

'Fuck you,' she said and turned away, irate.

'I'm sorry.'

'No, you're not.'

She was right. I wasn't in the least bit sorry. In fact, I felt nothing but monumental relief – like someone who thinks he's been driving an uninsured vehicle, but then discovers that he has no-fault insurance and can walk away from an accident unscathed. So I didn't offer up any more apologies for my tactless line of questioning, as I really wanted her to loathe me – in the hope that, having decided I was a four-star shit, she would immediately jettison me when we hit Broome. Keep 'em angry and they'll walk – that's rule number one of being an emotional hit-and-run artist.

Or, at least, I expected her to walk when we crossed the Broome town limits. It was just after sundown, not a word had been spoken between us for over three hours, and the atmosphere inside the microbus was downright combustible. I found a campsite a mile or two from the village centre, parked us in a quiet corner, put my hand on Angie's shoulder, and prepared to give her my standard 'It's Been Nice Knowing You . . . Have a Good Life' oration. But as I touched her, she suddenly grabbed me by my left arm and hauled me over the seat into the rear of the van. Here we go again . . . only this time there was no hint of affection as she rough-housed me to the floor. Instead, she sat on my chest, pinning my shoulders down with her knees. I wasn't exactly comfortable and when I attempted to budge, she pressed a clenched fist hard against my lips while her other hand went to work on my belt buckle.

'Don't you say a word,' she said, popping the buttons on my fly. 'Not one fucking word.'

Way back in 1977 – when I was on the news desk of the Raleigh *News and Observer* – I had great fun rewriting some UPI wire story about a crazed bimbo from Utah who became so infatuated with a Mormon missionary that she followed him to England and paid two stooges to kidnap him. Then, once she had him to herself in some remote rural cottage, she chained him naked to a bed, stuck a pistol to his head and said, 'Get it up, Brigham'. At the time, my fellow hacks made all sorts of jokes about that timid Mormon, noting that the bozo should have been grateful for such kinky treatment. But

I think we were all secretly appalled by this story. Because, at heart, most guys cannot handle the idea of a woman calling the sexual shots. Especially if she's brandishing a .38.

Angie wasn't brandishing anything but she was still scaring the shit out of me. Sex with her was like reliving the Sack of Gaul – you were pillaged and plundered in three action-packed minutes. She didn't make love, she mugged you. No finesse, no *tendresse*. She behaved like most men behave in the sack.

Granted, I knew there was something a little dangerous about her brand of amorous thuggery. But I have to admit that, in my own dumb male way, I was also flattered by such attention. I mean, it's not every day that a woman rolls over you like a bulldozer, or keeps nagging you to jump on her every two hours. So while a sensible little voice inside my brain whispered, 'Ditch the babe before it gets complicated', it was quickly drowned out by a bad boy who kept hissing stuff like, 'Only a spineless asshole would walk away from this kind of attention . . . Sit back and enjoy the party – especially since you can end it whenever you like.'

Naturally, I decided that the bad boy was the wiser counsellor – and therefore put up no resistance to Angie's onslaught. And after she fell off me with a primeval howl, I shelved my goodbye speech and said nothing disagreeable when she negotiated a détente between us.

'You still like me, don't you?' she asked, nuzzling up against me like a tom-cat.

I nodded, I smiled.

'No more domestics then, right?'

'Right.'

'We're going to hang together, yeah?'

I nodded again and now it was her turn to smile.

'I knew this would work,' she said. 'Knew it from the moment I saw you.'

I didn't like the sound of that – but I also figured: yeah, it'll work between us all right. Till next weekend anyway – when I finally push off again on my own.

And the funny thing was, the next few days really *did* work. In fact, they turned out to be, well . . . fun. Broome wasn't your usual Outback dump, but a curiously cosmopolitan place – an old fishing community where white Australians seemed to be outnumbered by the Malays and Polynesians who'd been running the pearling business there for the past hundred years. It was a town I understood – a tropical variation on a Maine seaport, with weatherbeaten houses, old nineteenth century trading outposts, decent bars and an indolent perspective on life. The sort of dump where everybody appeared to be perpetually hungover, where lack of productivity was considered a virtue and individual initiative meant cultivating five o'clock shadow. You never met the day before eleven and you squandered most of it at the beach – a mile-long shingle of hot white sand fronting the Indian Ocean.

Angie had never seen a beach before, never watched a breaker slam down upon a shoreline, never tasted the cold briny spray of sea water – and I couldn't help but enjoy her wide-eyed delight in this new sun-and-surf world. Though she'd been landlocked for the past twenty-one years, she showed an innate Australian aptitude for beach life. She spent our first full day in Broome studying the other couples along the shore and then marched us off to buy the requisite seaside gear: bamboo mats and frisbees and beachballs and loud Polynesian shirts and shitty Jackie Collins novels and an Esky heaped with ice-cold lager. We worked our way through a case of beer and three packs of Camels a day, sitting inanimate in the sand for nine hours with stacks of take-away food: fish-and-chips and satay sticks and Thai noodles and spring rolls and the occasional cheeseburger. Then – when the sun checked out – we'd waddle into town, pick up a bottle of cheap Riesling and some prawn curries at a Chinese carry-out, and stuff our faces while watching a movie at Sun Pictures – an outdoor cinema in the centre of Broome. Afterwards, we'd bung ourselves up with a couple of double-dip ice-cream cones, then head back to the van and bring ourselves to the brink of nausea with deranged aerobic sex.

Sun, sand, surf, sex, swill, satiation. Day in, day out, we practised gluttony. We gorged. We got fat. And we even began to like each other. Angie constantly surprised me. This might have been her first look at the world beyond Wollanup, but she refused to play the naïve bumpkin. If anything, she embraced modern life with ferocious aplomb . . . and she had opinions about everything. While buying all that beach gear, she had also picked up a Walkman and a dozen or so tapes, and immediately won my affection by rubbishing every contemporary ikon from Madonna ('Nothing but a blonde berk') to U2 ('Pretentious fucking wankers'). Once she'd seen three movies at Sun Pictures, she started talking as if she was Pauline Kael, bemoaning Kevin Costner's woodenness and Tom Cruise's tendency to smirk all the time ('Got a cute bum, though'). And after she spent an evening glued to CNN on a pub television, she said, 'It's pretty good . . . but why do they keep repeating the same bloody stories over and over again?'

She was also intuitive. Frighteningly intuitive. On our fifth night in Broome, we ended up on the beach after finally being evicted from some boozer at three in the morning. It was one of those electrifyingly clear evenings where the sky was putting on a show. The two of us were in an advanced state of alcoholic glee and we collapsed on the sand, trying to focus our eyes on the astral fireworks.

After a few minutes of silent Milky Way contemplation, Angie quietly said, 'You're going to dump me in a few days, aren't you?'

Immediately, I said, 'That's bullshit.' Immediately, I wondered, 'Am I that transparent?'

Angie didn't take her gaze away from the sky. 'It's not bullshit,' she said in the same composed voice. 'It's simply what you're going to do.'

'Come off it . . .'

'You do it all the time.'

'You don't know that.'

She gave me a cheerless smile. And said, 'Believe me, mate – it's written all over you. It's how you operate.'

I had no answer to that accusation – except 'Guilty as charged'. So I remained silent, losing myself even further in all that cosmic real estate. Until Angie brought me back to earth with one whispered word: 'Bastard.'

Before I could respond, she was on her feet, running down the beach. Our week of fun was over.

I knew she wanted me to do the expected thing and chase after her, but what could I say? Another bogus chorus of 'I'm so sorry'? Or that old break-up favourite, 'Let's be friends'? No way. This sort of fling has a limited shelf-life. You only get into it because you know that, after a week or so, it will have passed its sell-by date. And when that moment comes, it's dumb to postpone the inevitable and see if you can squeeze out a few more days. So I let Angie dart off into the night, figuring that we'd eventually meet up again at the van – where I'd finally get to deliver my bye-bye speech. A speech I really should have given a week ago.

But when I returned to the microbus, there was no sign of her. Still feeling under the sauce, I stretched out on one of the bunks. Five, maybe six hours evaporated. When I woke, Angie was sitting on the opposite bunk, her rucksack beside her. Her eyes were bruised with fatigue and had a curious glisten, hinting that she'd been crying.

'When'd you get back?' I mumbled, my brain still fogged in with sleep.

'An hour ago.'

'Didn't hear you.'

'You were zonked out, that's why.'

'Where'd you sleep?'

'The beach.'

'Shit.'

'Yeah, shit.' She stood up, hoisting her rucksack. 'You want me to go, don't you?'

56

'Angie . . .'

'None of your bullshit, Nick,' she said, her voice hard. 'Just a straight yes or no.'

I found myself staring at her legs, wondering if I could talk her into a valedictory quickie before pushing off. So I stretched out my arm and pulled her towards me. 'Come to bed,' I said.

'That's your answer?'

'Uh-huh.'

'You really want to be with me?'

'Yeah, I really do.'

'You sure now?'

'I'm sure.'

'That's good,' she said, peeling off her T-shirt. 'That's real good.'

Hungover and jaded, we didn't exactly tear each other apart in bed. Immediately afterwards, I dropped back off to sleep. Only this time I really seemed to be free-falling into some pitch-black coma-land – a place where, every so often, there was this blinding flashbulb-pop of light which momentarily illuminated some deeply strange tableau.

Like Angie binding my hands and feet with rope . . .

And filling a hypodermic needle from a little vial . . .

And jabbing the needle in my arm . . .

One weird dream. Only I'm sure I felt that nasty poke in the biceps before sky-diving back into darkness. Just as I'm also sure I heard the engine turn over. And the van pull out of the campsite. And the chassis shake-rattle-and-roll when we left the main road.

But then I was back in that deep, dark netherworld. And I stayed there for days. Happy and secure amidst all that nothingness.

Until I woke up.

part two

one

Nuclear war had been declared. The United States was squaring off against some crazed Arab dictator who was threatening to transform Hawaii into an Islamic republic. Already his Muslim warriors had captured Waikiki and were forcing hula-hula girls to wear the veil. A mass ritualistic burning of cocktail umbrellas had taken place on the beach and any restaurateur caught serving a Mai Tai was shot on sight. Possession of a Don Ho record was also a capital offence, and *samizdat* videos of *Blue Hawaii* were fetching a thousand dollars apiece on the black market. However, it was the *fatwa* against Jack Lord which finally snapped Washington's patience and they brought out the heavy artillery. A quartet of two-megaton missiles were launched from secret silos based within the Mormon Tabernacle in Salt

Lake City. But instead of hitting their predetermined targets in the Pacific, they went wildly off-course . . . and slammed into the side of my head.

Opening an eye was my first mistake. Sunlight hit the optic nerve, detonating a series of explosions. Shell fragments shattered every corner of my brain. Small flash fires broke out. A platoon of jackbooted soldiers were sent to quell the flames, but they simply poked at the blaze with their bayonets. And, all the while, an air raid siren howled between my ears.

Then I opened the other eye. The light was now so bright that my pupils felt as if they were being jabbed with sharp pencils. But when I slammed them shut, the nausea hit. A depth-charge collided with my gut and up came this ferocious projectile. It seemed to cascade for yards – a technicolour salvo of bile. The job done, I immediately passed out.

I don't know how long I was comatose this time – but when I came to I nearly lost my lunch again, as the stench of dried vomit engulfed the space where I lay. My face was also speckled with the remnants of my last supper in Broome (Thai noodles, I think), and my mouth tasted like a slop bucket. I wanted to bolt to the nearest shower, but when I tried to raise myself up, I found that I was completely devoid of any physical energy. And the strain of hoisting my head was so taxing that I blacked out once more.

And behold there came a voice. And the voice spake unto me: 'Fuck me, you chundered.'

Then came water. A Niagara of water. I was being hosed down – my face and body pummelled by the force of the spray. The walls and floor were also getting the car-wash treatment – and when I looked up, this liquid avalanche was so dense that I couldn't see who was wielding the hose.

The inundation ended, a door slammed and I was alone. Though still weak, the hose-down had at least cleared some smog from my brain and I could finally focus on my surroundings. I was in a tiny windowless shed – a box no bigger than a toilet cubicle, built out of rough-hewn wood with a low corrugated tin ceiling. Except for the old lumpy mattress on which I was sprawled and a tin bucket, the shed was empty – yet a smell of rotting poultry permeated the place. And the floorboards were speckled with dried crimson patches, hinting that a chicken or two might have taken its final walk in this cell.

I could just about handle the reek of dead hens. The heat was another matter. After Darwin and the road to Broome, I thought I was used to the barbecued climate of the bush. I thought wrong. Because this place was a microwave – a precooked inferno offering instant dehydration. Thankfully, someone had stripped me down to everything but my shorts before depositing me here, as I was sweating again within minutes of my dousing. But I was still too strung out to make it to my feet. How did I get so feeble?

Then I saw the large red welts on my wrists and ankles, the ugly purple bruise on my left bicep. Welts=rope/bruise=hypodermic needle. Just like my ga-ga dream.

Déjà vu, mate.

Suddenly I was scared. So scared I began to kick the side of the shed with my feet while screaming like a psycho.

The door burst open, I looked up and stared straight into another flash flood of water. It knocked me sideways off the mattress. After this short sharp blast, the same voice I heard earlier spoke again.

'Chill,' the voice said. 'Just chill right out.'

Standing in front of me was a short little guy around fifty, his grey hair pulled back in a ponytail, a pair of granny glasses hugging his nose. The lenses were chipped and smudged, the frames held together by old yellowing wads of masking tape. His cut-off denims also looked ragged and around twenty years old. So too did his moth-eaten Procul Harum T-shirt.

'The hell are you?' I said, the words slurring.

'I'm Gus,' he said. 'Angie's uncle.'

'Angie!' I yelled – another long deranged howl which only ended when Gus leaned over and slapped me across the face. Then crouching down beside me, he said, 'That's no way to sound off about your wife, mate.'

I felt panic punch my chest.

'Wife?'

'Yeah,' he said, tapping the little gold band now wrapped around my left ring-finger. 'Wife.'

I began to kick and scream, like some infant deep in the throes of a temper tantrum. My bad behaviour was rewarded with a second slap in the face from Gus.

'No use going troppo, Nick,' he said in a spacey laid-back voice. ' 'Cause everything's going to seem real mellow-yellow once the drugs wear off.'

'Drugs?'

'*Thorazine.* Known back where you come from as a Mickey Finn. Think she gave you two hundred milligrams every eight hours – at least that's what I told her to hit you with . . .'

'*You?*'

'I'm the, uh, chemist round here,' he said, a goofy little smile flickering across his lips. 'Sorry 'bout the bruise on your arm, by the way. She's a good kid, Angie, but she's bloody useless when it comes to using a hypo. Anyway, you've had around twenty three hundred mills of the stuff pumped into your bloodstream . . .'

'How much . . .?'

'Enough to keep you under for three and a half days. Which is why it's gonna take another twelve hours or so before you start feeling right.'

'I've been out for *three and a half days*?'

'That's what I said.'

'Where am I, goddammit?'

'Wollanup.'

A second panic punch to the chest.

'Angie's home town?' I asked.

'You got it.'

I shut my eyes, too frightened to say anything more. Gus must have smelt my fear, because he gave my right shoulder a hard reassuring squeeze and said, 'Lookit, mate – I know you're feeling a little loopy-in-the-head right now and you're also wondering what sort of gonzo scene you've found yourself in. But I promise that everything will be explained to you just as soon as you're back on your feet. In the meantime, my advice to you is lie back, relax and . . .' He reached into the pocket of his shorts, withdrew a can, and snapped off the ring-top. '. . . have a beer.'

'Fuck your beer,' I said.

He put the can down and brought his face close to mine, saying, 'Don't think you should talk that way to me, man.'

I spat at him, leaving a large wet teardrop of phlegm on his cheek. This insolence garnered me a third slap across the face. This time it hurt.

'I'm gonna pretend that didn't happen,' he said, wiping away the spittle with the tail of his T-shirt. 'Gonna blame it on the drugs Angie gave you and blank it right out of my brain. But if you do that again, you're gonna be pickin' up your teeth with broken fingers.'

'Why am I here?'

'Later, dude.' And he stood up.

'You're not leaving me . . .?'

'Got to get you detoxed before you get the big welcome.'

'Welcome from whom?'

'Your wife and family, of course.'

'Don't have a wife,' I shouted. 'Don't have a family.'

'Oh, yes, you do.' He opened the door. 'Back in a couple of hours,' he said.

'Heat's gonna kill me.'

'Nah, you'll live. Anyway, the more you sweat, the faster all that chemical gunk is gonna be out of your bloodstream. You start feeling bad, drink that beer I left you.'

'Please . . . wait . . .' I shouted.

65

But he was gone. And I was back in the dark. My mind on a crazed rampage. Spooked beyond belief. *Wife . . . family . . . Wollanup?* Sick joke, sick joke. Somebody please tell me this is all a sick joke.

two

The next twelve hours were not fun. I've often wondered what it must be like to detox from a vodka binge or take the cold turkey cure for heroin. I found out. First came the wet heaves. Then the dry ones. Then the shits. Then the shakes. Real Richter-scale shudders accompanied by night-sweats. The mattress became as sodden as a wet sponge, and I got hit with crazy hot/cold flashes. First, I was in the tropics, then in Alaska. The walls of the shed started to buckle, threatening to topple down over me. I clutched the bed in total terror, like someone trapped on a deranged roller-coaster. I was berserk, rabid, out of control. About to derail.

Whoosh.

Water. It hit me like buckshot. I raised my head and let it hammer my face, opening my mouth wide to kill the noxious thirst which had seized my throat. Through the deluge I could see Gus wielding the hose, his granny glasses fogged like swimming goggles.

'Get up,' he shouted over the water.

'Can't.'

'Yes, you can.'

'No . . .'

'Water's gonna run out in about two minutes. No water, no more shower. Your choice, mate.'

It was a major act of will, but I somehow managed to make it to my feet, balancing there precariously on legs as sturdy as Jell-O.

'Bra-fucking-vo,' Gus said. 'Now work yourself over with this.'

He tossed me a large brown bar of soap. It landed at my feet and I had to fight off the urge to crumple while picking it up. The soap was caked with grit and reeked of some medicinal substance that smelled potent enough to kill body lice. I built up a half-hearted lather, its antiseptic stench permeating the stubble on my face.

'Final rinse,' Gus said, working the spray up and down my torso. Then the water stopped. 'Dry yourself with this,' he said, throwing me a grubby towel no bigger than a dish-rag.

'Tell you, Nick-o, you're getting the right royal treatment. I mean, water's pretty scarce in Wollanup, so all these showers you've been having is kind of red carpet. But your wife was bloody insistent that we keep you feeling nice-and-fresh 'till you got over your little bout of the sicks. And you know Angie – gets her tits in a tangle if you don't do what she says.'

'I am *not* married,' I said.

Gus flashed me another of his stoned smiles. 'That's what we all say, man. You nearly dry?'

I nodded – even though the towel was uselessly scrawny and stank of leftover sweat. But anything that rag couldn't absorb, the heat took care of in seconds.

'Right, then, brought you some clean clobber.'

He handed me a small bundle. They were my clothes, all right: Fruit of the Loom jockeys, a white Gap T-shirt, a pair of khaki shorts and deck shoes from L. L. Bean. Looking at those American labels sent a little shudder through me. I could remember where and when I had bought each item: the T-shirt and the jockeys last May at the Maine Mall in Portland; the shorts and shoes at 3 a.m. on a June morning in '91, when I couldn't sleep and decided to kill the night by driving the fifty miles south from Augusta to Bean's 24-hour store in Freeport. My old life. Homesickness: the cruellest of aches if your exile is a self-imposed one. Or if you've landed yourself in a place beyond your understanding. Beyond logic. Way over your head.

'Where d'you find my clothes?'

'At your house, of course.'

'I don't have a house.'

'Angie wouldn't like to hear you say that, mate. Especially since she's fixed it up beaut for you.'

I spoke softly, imploringly. The words coming out with dull-witted slowness: 'Please. Tell me. Why. Am. I. Here?'

'Be cool and the mists will part real soon.'

'I want some fucking answers.'

'Patience, my man. And remember: you bring good vibes to the party, I promise you good vibes in return.'

Goddamn space cadet. Probably ate one magic mushroom too many, now thinks he's permanently on Haight and Fillmore. Try a little overhaul of your vernacular, asshole.

'Hurry up and get them clothes on,' Gus said. 'Everyone's waiting to meet you.'

As I dressed, Gus caught sight of the unopened can by the bed. 'Bugger it, you didn't drink the beer.'

'Too sick,' I said.

'Drink it now.'

'No, thanks.'

'You still feeling rough?'

'Real rough.'

'Can't blame you, with the bloody pong in here. That shit bucket looks pretty full to me.'

'You fucking surprised?'

'That negative karma ain't gonna win you mates, Nick-boy.'

'Piss on your karma. I want out of here.'

'Not until you toss back that beer.'

'Too sick.'

'You're gonna be sicker, if you don't chug-a-lug that lager. It's 120° out there – so you're gonna fall right over if you don't have something liquid inside you. You want out, you drink.'

I had no option but to do as ordered – especially since the prospect of further confinement in this chicken coop filled me with dread. So I popped the flip-top and guzzled it fast. The beer tasted like scalded soup. When it made contact with my empty stomach, I had to work hard at keeping it down. An extra layer of fuzz was added to an already clouded brain. Within seconds, I was stinko.

'Good on ya,' Gus said when I tossed the empty can into the shit bucket. 'You keep drinking like that, you're gonna fit in here just fine. Ready for the big welcome?'

'Guess so.'

'Terrif.'

He opened the door a few inches, shouted 'Comin' out now', closed it again and turned back to me. 'Okay, one last inspection,' he said, giving me the once-over. 'Hair's still a mess. Not that I care, man – but, y'know, first impressions kind of count for something, right?'

I ran my fingers a few times through the still-damp tangle. 'Better?' I asked.

'Just ace, mate. You're a bloody oil-painting.'

With a theatrical flourish, Gus threw open the door. Suddenly, the shed was overwhelmed by light. A blinding incandescence. The sort of Biblical light that would send a born-again Christian into rapture. Even pygmy Gus seemed to grow in stature when bathed in this celestial glow. And, assuming the role of Peter at the gates, he took me by the arm and said:

'Welcome to your new home.'

We walked into the light.

At first, I could see nothing. Four days of incarceration meant that my eyes couldn't handle the ultra-high wattage, so everything was a torturous blur. And my initial steps were so tentative, so shaky, that Gus had to wrap his arm around my waist in order to keep me upright. My lungs scrambled for fresh air, but instead breathed in charred oxygen – the atmosphere seared by the savage heat of the day and by a pernicious rankness. It seemed to be all-pervading, this stench – an *eau de cooked sewage* which delivered a knockout punch.

I became vaguely aware of a crowd – two dozen or so hard faces staring at me with sullen intensity. Their silence was so formidable, so distrustful, that I felt a bit like some condemned convict who'd drawn a mob for his final walk to the gallows. As my eyes began to adjust to the light, I could see a jumble of tie-dyed T-shirts, stringy hair, bell-bottoms, Old Testament beards, the occasional naked baby and a lot of bad dental work. What sort of time-warp commune was this? With jerry-built shacks lining a dirt road, a pack of emaciated dogs yelping at everybody's heels and – fuck me, this is impossible – a fifty-foot garbage mountain towering over this main drag. The source of the stench.

'Hey there.'

I knew that voice. I knew those big beefy arms encircling me. I knew that tongue-to-the-tonsils kiss and the rib-busting squeeze.

'How you doing, lover?'

I looked up at Angie. Her eyes were aglow with a chilling triumphalism.

'Ain't he neat?' she shouted to the crowd. 'Ain't he fab?'

She turned back to me, her face full of the sort of patronizing affection one usually reserves for the family pooch. 'My little hubby. My very own Yank.'

'Bitch,' I whispered. And passed out in her arms.

three

A bed. A big proper bed. With a soft mattress. And clean sheets. And feathery pillows. And, somewhere in the near distance, the aromatic scent of coffee and fried eggs in the air. Outside, a dawn chorus of kookaburras. Inside a different sort of antipodean hummingbird, singing an old showtune in a chirpy, jangling voice: '*I feel pretty, Oh so pretty, I feel pretty and witty and bright*!'

What fresh hell is this? First they put you in the chicken coop. Then in marriage?

'Morning, darl.'

Darl. As in *darling*. As in marital term of endearment.

It took a moment or two to get my bearings sorted out – to see where I had ended up this time after yet another trip down Coma Lane.

'Sleep well, darl?'

Actually, I had. Eight hours minimum. Drug-free too – if the relatively clear state of my head was anything to go by. For the first time in days, I felt like a near-operative member of the human race. Weak, but fog-free.

'Little cooked brekkie, darl?'

Yesterday, I would have gagged at the suggestion. This morning, though, I was ravenous.

'Fixed you two scrambled, toast and real coffee. But Gus says you got to eat everything real slow – 'cause you can't scoff solid tucker after four days of nothing but glucose and water – which is what we were keeping you alive on when you were unwell.'

Unwell? Try 'doped', sweetheart. Or 'shanghaied'. Had I not been so famished, I would have thrown the eggs in her face and demanded an explanation or two. But a little voice warned me to proceed with caution, to play along with her until I'd figured out this wacko scene. After all, if my 'wife' thought nothing of shooting me full of tranquillizers, abducting me, then keeping me locked up in a hen house until I was detoxed, it was safe to assume that she would consider other punitive measures if my behaviour displeased her. Best to do nothing provocative for the moment. Best to give the bitch a big appreciative smile and eat her rubbery eggs, cold toast, feeble coffee.

And how delighted she was to see me beam at her with such grateful affection. She beamed back as I ate – like some Suzy Homemaker type, whose only goal in life was to keep her Big Hubby happy.

'How's the coffee, darl?'

'Great,' I lied.

'Fresh coffee's considered a real delicacy in Wollanup – but I've been holding some for three years.'

Three-year-old coffee. No wonder it tasted so musty and insipid.

'And you know what I've been holding it for? This

moment. My first breakfast with my husband.'

'How nice,' I said.

'Real, real nice,' she said, snuggling up against me.

'Tell me about our wedding,' I said in a deliberately pleasant, neutral voice.

'Oh, it was just so beaut,' she said, her eyes brightening even more with romantic recollection. 'We held it in the pub and were married by my Daddy, who kind of serves as the justice of the peace around here. It was a white wedding, of course – with me in my Mum's old lace dress and you in this real handsome blue serge suit that we borrowed from my uncle Les. 'Course, you being sick, we had to bring you to the service in a wheelchair, which also meant that we couldn't stand during the ceremony. So we took the vows sitting next to each other.'

'And who said my vows for me?' I asked, maintaining the same matter-of-fact tone.

'Uncle Gus. He was your best man too. A great bloke, Gussie.'

I remembered his three slaps across my face, his threats of further bodily harm if I didn't behave myself.

'Yeah,' I said. 'Terrific guy.'

'Like your ring?' Angie asked. I nodded and glanced at the cheap piece of metal wrapped around my finger. With this keyring, I thee wed.

'A family heirloom?' I asked.

'Sort of,' Angie said. 'Belonged to my sister Krystal's husband.'

'Where's he now?'

Angie lowered her eyes. 'Uh . . . dead,' she said.

'Recently?'

'Two months ago.'

'Here in Wollanup?'

'Yeah.'

'What happened?'

Another evasive lowering of the eyes. 'Accident of sorts.'

'What's that supposed to mean?'

'What I said. He was involved in an accident.'

'What kind of accident?'

'Hunting.'

'You mean, an accident with a gun?'

'Right, he was shot with a gun.'

'Accidentally.'

A long silence before she answered. 'Yeah,' she said. 'It was all one big accident.'

'Your sister must be taking it pretty badly.'

'She's better now.'

'After only two months?'

'Well, she really didn't know him very long.' Angie immediately regretted that comment – and it showed, as she turned a flustered shade of red and dragged the conversation back into Harlequin Romance territory. 'Anyway, I had four bridesmaids dressed in pink chiffon and Gus's youngest son Ringo – he's only five – carried the rings . . . which everyone thought real cute, given his name and all. And there was fab party afterwards in the pub. Lots of piss and tucker. Must've drunk a dozen tinnies myself.'

'Was I there?'

'Nah, we had to put you back in the chicken coop, as you were starting to stir a bit and Gus was worried you might've gone mental if you came to at your own wedding.'

'Very thoughtful of him.'

'But I saved you a piece of wedding cake. Chocolate and treacle, made by my aunt Ruthie. Want it now?'

'No thanks.'

'Really wish you could've seen the whole celebration.'

'So do I. Any photos?'

'Nah.'

'That's surprising.'

'Yeah, I really wanted some. But . . . no cameras in Wollanup.'

'Why not?'

'Banned 'em.'

'No way.'

'Yep – taking photos is against the law here.'

'Whose law?'

'Our law.'

'But that's crazy . . .'

'Like I told you when we first met, Australian laws ain't Wollanup laws.'

I was about to ask her if Wollanup laws also sanctioned abduction and shotgun weddings where the groom was unconscious. Once again, though, I reined myself in before losing it completely. I mean, I really couldn't believe what I was hearing – and I wanted to scream and shout and insist she call an end to this warped charade. But watching her eyes go all dreamy as she calmly related all the frilly details of our narcotic nuptials, I knew this was no elaborate prank she was pulling. She had snarled me into a game called 'Playing House' – and I sensed that she expected me to play it seriously and by her rules. Wollanup rules.

'Darl,' she said, taking both my hands and looking at me squarely in the eyes, 'I know it's gonna take you a while to adjust to how we do things here. Being so far away from everything means that we kind of have our own customs and values, which might strike an outsider as fucked-in-the-head, but which suit us fine. So please, give the place a chance – 'cause I want you to be happy here. And also because . . .' She hesitated, choosing her words carefully. '. . . I don't want you to be like certain other newcomers who didn't adjust. Which meant that things didn't work out too well for 'em. But that's not gonna be you, yeah?'

What else could I do but smile a dumb smile and assure her I'd adapt.

'Oh, you are one beaut bloke,' she said, grabbing me in an affectionate headlock. 'We're gonna have fun together, aren't we?'

'Lots of fun,' I said.

'And you know what we're gonna do for the next three days?'

'What?'

'We're gonna have ourselves a honeymoon.'

'Whereabouts?'

'Right here, of course. In bed. For the next seventy-two hours, I'm gonna jump you like a rattlesnake. And I expect no resistance, get me?'

'Loud and clear,' I said, sounding very nervous.

four

Thankfully, Angie quickly forgot her threat to keep me in bed for seventy-two hours. Nor did she turn our 'honeymoon' into the non-stop sexual gymkhana I feared. As long as we fell on top of each other three times a day (preferably before mealtimes), she was happy. Though I found this thrice-daily schedule arduous, I didn't resist any of her advances. My immediate short-term aim was to keep her sweet and build up some harmonious trust between us before figuring out my next move. And if this meant feigning passion three times a day, so be it. I was a kept man, after all. A hostage husband. And since she held all the cards right now, I knew that fighting with my captor was pointless.

Getting to know you,
Getting to know all about you,
Getting to like you,
Getting to hope you'll like me . . .

Angie played that damn song over and over again on her record player during our little indoor holiday, singing along with the scratchy voice of Gertrude Lawrence from the original Broadway cast recording of *The King and I*.

'Where d'you get a hold of that collector's item?' I asked as she lifted the tone arm to cue the song again.

'Wedding gift from Gus. He's got dozens of old records over at his place. Gave us this and the soundtrack to *West Side Story*. Nice tunes, but the story's a real downer, innit?'

'Well, it is supposed to be Romeo and Juliet.'

'Who?'

'Romeo and Juliet?'

'Nah, nah, nah – the lovers are called Tony and Maria.'

'But they're based on Romeo and Juliet.'

'Never heard of 'em.'

When I am with you
Suddenly it's bright and cheery
Because of all the beautiful and new
Things I'm learning about you
Day by day.

Not only did Angie play that number at least six times a day, she also made a point of putting her arms around my neck, showgirl-style, while serenading me with it.

'That's our song,' she said, coercing me into two-stepping to the melody. As we danced, I couldn't help but wonder if all this lovey-doveyness was part of some calculated plan to soften me up and lull me into accepting my 'arranged' marriage. Because, at heart, Angie was about as lovey-dovey as a linebacker – a big bruiser of a tomboy who liked to guzzle beer and break wind. So why had she suddenly transformed herself into a bad facsimile of a Stepford Wife – always bringing me breakfast in bed, baking cakes, massaging my feet, fetching my slippers, saying cringe-making things like 'I'm your sex slave', singing her dumb showtunes, and calling our home 'the love nest'.

Not that this 'nest' exuded much in the way of romance. On the contrary, it was a hovel. A tiny one-room shack with bare chipboard walls and a tin roof which sounded like a thousand snare drums whenever there was a freak flash of rain. The floor was grey concrete – an unevenly laid surface that was so rough on the feet it removed all my accumulated callouses. A strip of Axminster carpet covered a small area in front of a coral green plastic couch – an instant butt-sauna which retained the Outback heat and was therefore impossible to sit on. An old red corduroy beanbag was the only other object of furniture in the room, but collapsing into it meant stomaching its distinctive old dog odour. Behind one set of bead curtains was the kitchen/dinette (a sink, a hot-plate, a tiny fridge, a collapsable card-table and two green metal folding chairs); behind the other was our big mushy bed – comfortable so long as neither of us rolled into the mattress's hollow midsection. A blanket nailed to a door-frame masked the latrine – a shower stall and a chemical toilet that had to be emptied once a week. For entertainment, there was Angie's six-book library of doctor/nurse romances, her stack of old 45s, the two musical soundtracks and nothing else.

'Ain't it ripper, our little place?' Angie said, pulling me closer as we continued to dance to the velvety voices of Yul Brynner and Gertrude Lawrence.

'Yeah. Really tasteful.'

'You'll have to tell Daddy how much you like it when you meet him. Built it for us as a wedding gift.'

'For *us*?'

'Well, for me and whatever husband I eventually came back with?'

'You mean, you were travelling around, *looking* for a husband?'

She stiffened in my arms. 'Course I wasn't,' she said. 'I simply met you and knew right away that you were the one.'

'I see.'

My curt tone evidently angered her, as she pulled away from me and gave me a hard, threatening look.

'You don't believe me, do you?' she said.

Danger zone, danger zone.

'I do believe you, Angie.'

'Then don't go asking me any more fruit-loop questions like that.'

'Sorry.'

'This is our honeymoon, and I don't want it spoiled.'

The Stepford Wife had transformed herself back into the redneck I knew and feared.

'How about a walk?' I said.

'We don't need no bloody walk,' she said, the anger now showing.

'Just a suggestion, that's all.'

'Stupid shit-wit suggestion.'

'Okay, forget it.'

'You want to take a fucking walk, you fucking well wait until the fucking honeymoon's over and you can take as many fucking walks as you like.'

She was screaming, I was spooked. Spooked by this Jekyll and Hyde act – and how little it took to make her go apeshit.

'Angie, please . . .' I said, trying to calm her down. But she kept prowling up and down the room like a seething cat.

'Dickhead Yank, bloody ruin everything don't you? Try to make a nice home, nice life for you, you wanna walk. Kill you, I could. Fucking tear your fat Yank face. Fucking . . .'

I grabbed her by the shoulders and shook her hard.

'All right, all right, enough,' I shouted, but she was out of control and began to shove me with her hands, shrieking, '*Not enough, not enough, not enough* . . .'

Then she punched me. Twice. Once in the left eye. Once on the nose. The second blow sent me across the room. I landed on the sofa, my nostrils dripping blood on to the hot plastic cushions.

A strange quiet settled across the room – the same sort of unreal quiet that follows a car crash. Then came a flood of tears and remorse.

'Oh God, oh God, oh God, oh God, oh God,' she wailed and was all over me, rocking me in her arms, sobbing into my chest while blood blotted her T-shirt. As the real guilt hit, she started to howl, 'WhydidIwhydidIwhydidIwhydidI . . . ?' . . . echoing it over and over again, as if it was some sort of insane act of contrition.

The 'sorries' followed. There must have been two dozen of them, repeated with the same deranged anguish that accompanied the *whydidI?* mantra. I once read somewhere that wife-beaters often pull this routine – after popping their partner in the face, they get down on their knees and beg forgiveness. I knew Angie wanted me to accept her hysterical apology, but I was too numb with shock to say anything. Until, that is, the pain arrived.

'Get some ice,' I said quietly.

She raced to the fridge, nearly tearing off the door while rifling through the little freezer compartment. After a moment she turned back to me, shaking her head, panic-stricken. 'No ice,' she said.

'Cold meat, then.'

She started cleaving the fridge apart again and this time was successful, holding up a foot-long chunk of frozen blue flesh.

'What is it?' I asked.

' 'Roo steak.'

'*Kangaroo* steak?'

'Yeah. Saving it for dinnies tonight.'

'That all we got?'

She nodded, anxiously waiting my command.

'Then bring it here. And get me something to mop up this blood.'

She raced back to me with the steak and a grubby dishtowel speckled with dried egg. I moved to the beanbag, plugged my nostrils with two corners of the towel, then draped the frozen 'roo steak over my injured nose and eye. Angie was immediately at my side, cradling my head, still having a bad attack of the boo-hoo-hoos.

'I don't know what to say . . .'

'Say nothing.'

'You'll never forgive me.'

Goddamn right I won't. Because you're a nut, babe. A psycho in full spring bloom. And the only thing stopping me from rearranging your face is the probable price I would have to pay for inflicting such damage. Your bed is still preferable to the interior of that fucking chicken coop. And maybe I can capitalize on your guilt to get a question or two answered.

'I'll forgive you,' I lied.

Her face immediately lightened. 'Really? You mean that?'

'Yeah. But . . . I need to know something.'

'Anything. What?'

I took a deep, steadying breath. And asked: 'Why am I here?'

She looked at me, bemused. 'I don't understand?' she said.

'What am I doing here? With you. In Wollanup.'

'We're . . . married. That's why you're here.'

I chose my next words with considerable care. 'But . . . I didn't want to get married.'

'That's not true,' she said, all upset. 'You proposed.'

This was news to me.

'When?' I demanded.

'In your van. After we had that barney and I spent the night on the beach, remember? And I came back at dawn and asked if you wanted me to leave. And what did you do?'

It was all coming back to me now, with unfortunate clarity. 'I pulled you into bed,' I said.

'*Right*. But before I got under the sheets with you, I asked again if you really really *really* wanted to be with me. And you said a very clear, very definite *yes*. So there you go, mate.'

'That wasn't a marriage proposal,' I said, an edgy desperation in my voice.

'What d'you call it then?'

A dumb fool seduction line, actually. Why, oh, why did I chase after one last bonk?

'I just didn't want to end things so abruptly.'

'That's not what you said. That's not what you promised.'

'I promised you *nothing*.'

'As far as I'm concerned, when you said you really really really wanted to be with me, you made a commitment. *To me*. Anyway, the first day I met you, you said you wanted a wife, a family.'

'Wait a minute . . .'

'You *did*. I can recall the moment exactly. You told me how your parents were dead and you had no relatives. I said, "Would you like to belong to a family, a community?" and you got this real sad little boy look on your face and told me you'd never been given the chance.'

The little boy look. It wasn't meant to be a plea for adoption.

'Listen, Angie,' I said, 'there's obviously been a crazy misunderstanding.'

A very poor choice of words. That malevolent look crossed her face again.

'There is nothing crazy about this, Yank. You wanted a family, you proposed marriage, I accepted and brought you here. End of bloody story.'

'You drugged me . . .'

'You were unwell in Broome . . .'

'. . . wasn't . . .'

'You *were*, mate. So sick you couldn't get out of your bunk in the van. So I gave you some medicine, you had a bad reaction to it and went blotto for three days – which meant I had to do all the bloody driving down here.'

'And the wedding?'

'We got here, you were still sick, all the preparations were made, so we decided to go ahead with it.'

'Even though I was out cold?'

'That's right.'

Now it was my turn to lose it.

'You really expect me to believe such crazy shit?' I yelled.

'Watch it . . .'

'Snatch me outta Broome, marry me without my consent, and then try to justify it by spinning some crap about how I was proposing to you in some coded goddamn way? All I wanted to do was bed you, Angie. Understand? Get in your pants and jump your bones. Nothing more, you sick . . .'

I never got to finish that sentence, as Angie interrupted it with another fast jab to my nose. It sent the meat flying and kickstarted the haemorrhage in my nostrils. Instant agony – and I howled. Angie – her hands trembling – became all businesslike. Finding a new dishrag to staunch the flow of blood. Helping me on to the bed. Rearranging the frozen steak on my battered nose and eye. Handing me two aspirin and a lukewarm can of beer. Turning on her record player, dropping the needle on *The King and I*, and singing along to 'We Kiss in the Shadow'.

> *'To kiss in the sunlight*
> *And say to the sky*
> *Behold and believe what you see,*
> *Behold how my lover loves me.'*

We said nothing to each other for the rest of the night. I swallowed the aspirin, drank the beer and rode the pain until sleep finally whisked me away.

When I woke in the dawn's early light, the entire upper half of my face felt paralysed. But though my, nostrils were

clogged with dried blood, my sense of smell was still functioning, as the aroma of fried food floated in from the kitchen
area. Hearing me stir, Angie waltzed over and gave me an
enormous kiss on my lips.

'Morning, darl,' she chirped, her eyes bright with that
eager-to-please newly-wed glow. 'And how's my big old
hubby this morning?'

She wants to pretend nothing happened. No fights, no
blows, no blood, no responsibility for past events. Today is the
first day of the rest of your life. In Wollanup. Smile and try to
get through it in one piece.

'I'm good. Real good.'

'Little cooked brekkie, darl?'

'Sure. What you making?'

' 'Roo steak,' she said.

five

The rest of the honeymoon was an unqualified success. Not a crossed word, not a raised fist, not a black eye between us. And never once did I suggest we take a walk. Instead, we lolled about our 'love nest', playing at Just Marriedhood.

There was, however, one tricky moment when I delicately mentioned the word 'contraception' and expected to get my teeth loosened for such effrontery. But Angie was surprisingly calm after I broached the issue.

'Got the all-clear while you were unwell. Which means we've got ourselves another danger-free week before we start having to take precautions. So you see, darl – no worries. No worries at all.'

'Getting to Know You' continued to receive substantial

airtime on Angie's record player, but I was able to intersperse a few sixties hits between these marathon replays of Rodgers and Hammerstein – though every time I spun an old dumb song from my youth, like 'Bus Stop' or 'Sloop John B', it only served to unnerve me – to slam home my displacement.

'Want to hear a beaut tune?' Angie said, dropping another disc on the turntable. A classic opening bass solo blared through the tinny little loudspeaker, followed by the sandpaper voice of Eric Burdon, and I had to smile. The song was that ancient hit for The Animals, 'We Gotta Get Outta This Place'.

Angie, noticing my grin, said, 'Old favourite of yours?'

'New favourite,' I said, but she didn't catch the irony. Instead, in her eagerness to please me, she kept playing it almost as compulsively as her *King and I* highlights – which was fine by me. 'We Gotta Get Outta This Place' became my theme song, my anthem, my immediate agenda.

'Tucker time!'

This became another feature of our daily routine. After each of our three daily excursions between the sheets, Angie would make a post-coital spring from the bed to the kitchen, emerging an hour or two later to shout, 'Tucker time!' in a sing-songy voice. I came to dread this cutesy feeding call almost as much as Angie's toxic cooking. Not that her lack of culinary skill was totally to blame, as she had to make do with the limited foodstuffs on offer in Wollanup – none of which (bar the locally hunted 'roo meat) was fresh.

'No such thing as proper produce in Wollanup,' she said. 'Milk and eggs are both powdered. No cows here, so no butter or cheese. No real veggies – just tinned carrots, beans, tomatoes and corn. You sick of 'roo meat, you gotta make do with either Spam or tinned corned beef. Tinned pineapples or prunes are the two fruits on offer. And if you can't stomach the local spring water, you better like the amber – 'cause beer is the only drink they bring in.'

I now understood why Angie's eggs tasted so ersatz, and

why the water had such a metallic, mineral tang. But Tucker time! still remained a dreaded adventure, due to Angie's well-meaning attempts at inventiveness with the paltry supplies on offer. She'd spend hours hovering over the hot-plate, then announce (with considerable ceremony) her specialty *du jour*.

'You're gonna love this, darl. 'Roo steak fried in beer batter with a chunky pineapple glaze.'

'Sounds wonderful,' I'd say weakly.

'Tried something new for brekkie this morning. A Spanish omelette.'

'What's in it?'

'Spam, carrots, powdered eggs.'

'My, my.'

'And this being the last night of our honeymoon, I'm doing something real special for dinnies. Baked corned beef and prunes flambé.'

'You are amazing.'

Tucker time! To hell with my battered face – this culinary freak-show was the real agony of the honeymoon. And I was hoping against hope that, as soon as we settled down into day-to-day domesticity, Angie would either weary of such mind-bending creativity in the kitchen or (better yet) let me take charge of meals.

Not, of course, that I was planning to dig myself into this domestic scene for very long. Once I was finally allowed out of the house and could properly suss Wollanup, I'd start working on a way to vanish quietly in the middle of the night. Already, though, there was a little problem impeding my potential get-away: my money and passport had gone missing.

I discovered this on the last day of the honeymoon – when I was finally allowed access to the rest of my clothes. Up until that point, Angie was rather vague about the where-abouts of my personal effects, and insisted on hand-washing my T-shirt, shorts and jockeys every night before we went to bed, then leaving them on the plastic sofa to dry by morning. Of course I found this laundry situation weird, but I was getting used to weirdness as a norm – and in the interest of maintaining a certain détente between us, didn't question it for the time being.

That is, until I managed to 'accidentally' dump half of Angie's corned beef and prune concoction down my front, thereby relieving me of the obligation to finish it.

'That was clever,' she said, standing up. 'Get you some clean clobber.'

'My stuff is here?'

'Sure,' she said, reaching beneath the bed and pulling out the small footlocker where I had stored all my gear in the van. 'Been here all the time.'

'You didn't tell me you'd brought that in.'

'You didn't ask, mate.'

She flipped open the top and there, indeed, were all my clothes. I stripped off my soiled garments, found another pair of shorts and a T-shirt, and did a quick inventory to make certain the rest of my effects were still present. They were – bar the passport and the wad of traveller's cheques I had hidden at the bottom of the locker.

'Uh, Angie, I hate to say this, but something's missing.'

'Passport and money, right?'

'You've got them?'

'Nah, gave 'em to my Uncle Les.'

'Why?'

'Well, he's the banker in town.'

'There's a bank in Wollanup?'

'Just a safe – but Les is in charge of it. Anyway, it's all under lock and key, so there's nothing to sweat. But, hey, you didn't tell me you were so bloody rich. Six and a half thousand American dollars. That's quite a bit of dosh.'

'That's all the money I have in the world.'

'Well, with Les looking after it, it's real secure. Anyway, we don't use money in Wollanup.'

'You *don't*?'

'Nah – everything runs on the chit system. You'll see how it operates tomorrow – after you knock off work.'

'I'm going to work?'

'Didn't Gussie tell you? You're gonna be helping Daddy at his garage. Your van's there right now, by the way.'

'What's it doing there?'

'Developed a couple of mechanical problems on the way down here. But don't worry – Daddy's sorting 'em out.'

'He knows what he's doing?'

Angie looked at me, appalled. 'Daddy's the best,' she said.

There was a knock at the door.

'Company!' Angie chirped, opening it. It was Gus – still dressed in the same cruddy cut-off denims, but with a faded Rolling Stones-at-Altamont T-shirt now drooping across his emaciated chest.

'How are the peace-and-lovebirds?' he asked.

'Just beaut,' Angie said, handing him a can of lager. While cracking it open, he caught sight of my shiner and my red distended nose.

'Looks like you had a hell of a honeymoon, mate,' he said, elbowing me in the ribs.

'Yeah,' I said, 'hell of a honeymoon.'

'It was real great,' Angie chimed in, grabbing my neck in a bear-lock.

'Well, hate to spoil the party,' Gus said, 'but they want to see you now.'

'Who's "they",' I asked.

'The town council,' Gus said. 'That's me and the three other heads of the families in town. We're sort of the welcoming committee around here.'

'You'll get to meet Daddy,' Angie said.

'Yeah, he's real interested in getting to know his son-in-law,' Gus said. 'And after we're done, uh, welcoming you, you'll have the chance to down a few with everyone else in Wollanup, 'cause we're having our monthly town meeting in the boozer.'

'And I get to show you off to everyone, darl.'

'Will this guy Les be part of the welcoming committee?' I asked.

'Natch,' Gus said. 'He's the head of one of the families.'

'Good – I want to ask him about the banking arrangements in town.'

Gus tried to suppress a smirk. And said, 'I'm sure he'll tell you everything you want to know on that subject. You right, then?'

'Don't I need to get changed?' I asked, thinking that I might want to look a bit sprucer before meeting my in-laws. Once again, Gus found my question deeply amusing.

'Hell, mate, by Wollanup standards you're already dressed formal.'

Angie gave me a big hug and muttered something melo-dramatic about this being our first separation since getting married. I said I was sure we'd cope and felt monumental relief when Gus opened the front door and pushed me through it. The honeymoon was well and truly over. I was no longer confined to quarters.

It was around six at night – that time of day in the bush when the sun looks like a knob of butter in a red hot skillet – liquid and sizzling and caramelizing into a golden brown. I took a deep lungful of air and instantly regretted it, as I was reintroduced to the stench of the garbage mountain. I could see it in the near distance, towering over the diminutive Wollanup townscape.

'Nice pong, innit?' Gus said as I wheezed and coughed.

'How can you stand it?'

'You'll get used to it. Anyway, in a couple of weeks we're torching the lot. Kind of a quarterly event – set fire to the rubbish-tip and have us a barbie.'

'Ever thought about burying your garbage, instead of let-ting it pile up like that?'

'Ground's too bloody hard. And as y'see, we're kind of hemmed in here by Mother-fucking-Nature.'

I followed his hand as he pointed to the horizon and

straightaway succumbed to despair. For Wollanup wasn't simply 'hemmed in' by topography – it was actually imprisoned by it; a town held hostage by a sadistic landscape.

We were in a valley, a deep arid depression in the earth, encircled by high cliffs of flaky blood-red shale. These baked crimson bluffs encircled the valley, like a vast turret on some prehistoric castle. Were you to perch atop these cliffs and look down the three hundred feet into the chasm below, you might just think: this is, verily, the last place on earth. A sun-scorched abyss. A pit without egress. But when you stood at the epicentre of that pit, gazing up at those red battlements, you almost felt mocked by this menacing terrain – as if the topographical gods were looking down on you and saying, 'Try getting out of this one, sucker.'

My shock was palpable – like a felon who, after a long journey in the dark, finally glimpses the true severity of his maximum security prison. Gus was assuming the role of the warden – silently gauging my level of consternation as I came to terms with my shrunken circumstances. I could sense he was almost reading my jumbled, panicky thoughts. Following my eyes as they scanned the terrain, looking for potential points of escape. Watching me study the one red dirt road that bisected the village – a road which snaked its way up into the hills at the far end of town. Hearing the little voice inside my head whisper to me, 'That's the way out of here.'

He knew what I was going through, all right. So much so that when he said, 'Let's walk', he did so in a quiet, almost commiserating tone. Preparing me for further jolts ahead.

When they had finally let me out of the chicken coop and I had a moment or two of blinkered, sun-dazzled consciousness before collapsing into Angie's waiting arms, I had got the impression that I was in something of a jerry-built town – a thrown-together community. But nothing really could have prepared me for the abhorrent reality of Wollanup. The true vileness of it all.

Let's begin with the road. Unpaved red clay – an obstacle

course of ditches and potholes. Dog shit everywhere. Trash everywhere – as any heavy objects that didn't make it to the garbage mountain were simply left to rot on the side of this thoroughfare. There were old fridges, and battered armchairs dappled with bird droppings, and a disused toilet, and half-torn bags of cement, and rusted bits of cars, and – this was unbelievable – around a half-dozen or so kangaroo heads. They were in assorted stages of decomposition and all of them appeared to have been preyed upon by the packs of dogs that roamed the town – a platoon of rangy wild-eyed mutts, saliva dripping from their fangs as they yelped and growled and fought over another chunk of entrail.

Our house was at the far end of the road – the last stop before it petered out into a wide-open plateau of hard gravelly dirt. This tableland extended for a good two miles and then dead-ended against the rocky ramparts of the hills that encased Wollanup. There were three other shacks in various stages of construction opposite us – but this was the outer suburbs, as the majority of dwellings were grouped together in one large cluster a quarter-mile down the road. Every house was built in the same low-rent style – unpainted walls of flimsy fibreboard, a tin roof, a tiny lip of a porch hammered together from knotty, cheap lumber, a cement latrine out back. The shanty town look. Early Appalachia.

Beyond these shacks was the 'commercial' centre of town. The schoolhouse was an open-air shed with a dozen desks and a blackboard. The power station was a concrete bunker adjacent to the garbage mountain. The general store was a prefabricated box of aluminium siding. So too was the largest building in town: a long narrow warehouse with a badly hand-painted sign – Wollanup Meats – slapped on its front.

And then there was the pub. By Wollanup standards, it was an historic building. And, at two floors, the only sky-scraper in town. With whitewashed timber siding. A proper slate roof. A sun portico supported by a pair of wrought-iron columns. A horseshoe-shaped bar of polished wood, behind which were big built-in steel fridges. A couple of old electric beer-signs and a stuffed kangaroo head shared a wall with a large upside-down Australian flag. Up a wobbly flight of stairs, there was a small office with a steel desk, a steel chair, a steel safe, a steel filing cabinet and three large men waiting to greet me.

'Well, here's the bloody Yank,' Gus said as we entered the room. 'Fresh from his honeymoon. Nice job she did on his headlamps and his beak, eh?'

Not a smile from this trio. Like Gus, they were all around fifty. Unlike him, they bordered on the Neanderthal – three hefty gorillas, all over 300 lbs, all making me, at just six feet, feel like a midget.

'This here's Robbo,' Gus said, pointing to a guy with kango-hammers for hands and a large hairy wart sprouting out of his forehead. 'Runs our meat processing business.'

A grunt from Robbo.

'And Les . . .' Four teeth left in his mouth, a drinker's bulbous nose, a face like a penicillin culture . . . 'takes care of the general store and is also the town's treasurer.'

'Gidday,' he said tonelessly.

'And finally, your father-in-law. Daddy.'

He must have been six-five. All brawn. Wearing a pair of dungarees and no shirt. A mutant cauliflower for a head. Tree-trunks for arms. Dark, impervious eyes. And a handshake which left me begging for physiotherapy.

'So,' he said slowly, 'you're the bastard.'

I smiled feebly – and kept my mouth shut, awaiting further developments.

'Cat got your tongue, mate?' he said.

'No . . . sir.'

'Then answer my bloody question.'

'What question?'

'"So you're the bastard who was poking my daughter up in Broome" . . . that question.'

'Uh, I guess . . .'

'Whaddaya mean, y'guess? You don't *know* if you were poking her?'

This was not going at all well.

'No, I know all right.'

'Good poke, my Princess?'

'Sir, please . . .'

'Please what?'

'We're, uh, married now.'

'Fucking right, you are. I even remember the wedding – which is probably more than you can, eh?'

Howls of laughter from the quartet.

'Princess tells me you're a journo,' Daddy continued.

'That's right.'

'Ain't much use for a journo in Wollanup. No newspaper . . . and hardly anybody can read.'

More spontaneous guffaws. They really were enjoying themselves.

'But Princess also says you know a thing or two about wheels. True?'

'Suppose so. Serviced my own car back in the States and the van I bought here.'

'How much you pay for that putt-putt?'

'Twenty-five hundred.'

Exclamations of disbelief were followed by further glee.

'Two-Five-O-O for an old fuck-truck?' Daddy said, shaking his head. 'You really got done.'

'Made it from Darwin to here, didn't it?'

'Yeah, but it's one big dud now. Carbie's buggered and two of the valves are clapped out. Other than that, it's ace. Anyway, first thing tomorrow you can get to work fixing it – 'cause my Princess asked that I find you something to do in my garage. Think she decided you were a little too Yank sissie for what she does all day.'

'What's that?'

'You mean she didn't tell you . . . and you didn't ask? What've the two of you been doin' for the past couple of days?'

Cue ribald laughter.

'Princess – like just about everyone else in Wollanup – works in the meat-processing plant. Our only industry; our only source of revenue. The reason this town stays alive.'

Robbo came in here.

'Dab hand with a cleaver, your missus,' he said. 'I'd watch that, if I were you.'

I really was a laugh-a-minute to these guys.

'Ever butcher a 'roo, mate?' Robbo now asked.

'Uh . . . no.'

'Want t'learn, come by the plant. 'Cause that's what we do all day. Turn dead 'roos into pet food. Lot of fun.'

'Don't think that's your idea of fun, is it, Journo?' Daddy said. 'Don't think any of this strikes you as much fun, now, does it?'

I stayed silent.

'Cat got your tongue again, Journo? Or do I take your lack of a reply to mean that you're pleased as punch to be here?'

'No,' I said, my voice hoarse. 'I am not pleased.'

Daddy flashed me a malicious grin.

'Honesty at last. And I'm real real sorry to hear of your, uh, discomfort. But, hey, all I can say to you in reply is . . . stick it up your arse, mate. You poked her once, you poked her twice, you kept on poking her . . . now you live with the consequences. Princess, as you might have noticed, kind of takes these things seriously. Which means so do I. Personally speaking, I can't figure out what she sees in a fuck-wit like you. But you proposed and she accepted and now . . .'

Without thinking, I blurted out, 'I did *not* propose.' A very bad move – as Daddy turned to his trio of mates, shook his head sombrely, then turned back to me with murder in his eyes.

'You didn't say that, did you?'

'No,' I croaked, 'I didn't.'

'Louder, please.'

'I Did Not Say That.'

'You proposed, she accepted – was that the correct order of events?'

I momentarily hesitated.

'Was it?' he bellowed in my ear.

'Absolutely.'

'Good – because if it wasn't, you'd be saying that my Princess was a liar. Which, of course, she isn't, right?'

'Right.'

'You're the fucking liar.'

'I'm the liar.'

'Very good. Think we're starting to understand each other. Don't you think so too?'

'Yes. I do.'

'Then listen good to what I am about to tell you. There are only three things you really have to understand about Wollanup. The first is that, as Princess probably told you, there are just four families in town and we are the heads of them. We don't got a government. We don't got cops, we don't got no courts, and we certainly don't got no fucking lawyers. The four of us run the show. Make the rules. And punish the shit-wits.

'The second thing you should know is that the next town is a sixteen-hour drive from here down an unsealed track. In other words, we are so far from anything we might as well not exist. And as far as any of those bloody galahs in Perth or Canberra are concerned, we really don't exist. This place is off the map.

'And the final thing you should understand about Wollanup is this: we take a very dim view of, uh, marital abandonment. So if you try to run away, we'll barbie your goolies. Slowly. Any questions?'

I felt as if I had been punched in the solar plexus. All I wanted to do was curl up in a corner with my arms over my head and pretend that none of this was happening. Daddy was not pleased with my lack of response.

'I said: you got any questions?'

I bit my lip and could feel my eyes begin to water. I was snared. Ambushed. Trapped. Lost.

'No, sir,' I said through my tears. 'No questions at all.'

Les finally spoke. 'Believe the Yank's a bit blue, Daddy. Believe he's having an attack of the boo-hoo's.'

'Ain't that a shame,' Daddy sang. And the others laughed.

'Didn't you have a question for Les here?' Gus asked. 'A question –' snigger-snigger '– about banking?'

Les was all smiles. 'You were wondering about your money, Yank?'

I nodded.

He knelt down by the grey steel safe and spun the dial a few times before opening it. 'Got it all right here,' he said, tossing the pile of traveller's cheques on to the desk. 'Got your passport here too.' Opening up my blue identity document, he read the first page out loud: '*The Secretary of State of the United States of America hereby requests all whom it may concern to permit the citizen named herein to pass without delay or hindrance and in case of need to give all lawful aid and protection.*' He slammed it shut and said, 'Don't think the US have established diplomatic ties with Wollanup, have they, Gus?'

'Not that I heard.'

'Too bad for you, Yank,' Les said. 'Looks like that "pass without delay" bullshit doesn't apply here.' He tossed the passport in my face. 'You can hold on to this, if y'like. Not that you'll be needing it again. And count those traveller's cheques while you're at it.'

'No need,' I said.

'Count 'em,' Les barked. 'I insist.'

I did as ordered, sitting behind the big steel desk. It took several minutes, as there were sixty-five hundred-dollar Amex cheques. All present and accounted for.

'Happy?' Les said.

'Yes.'

'Ripper. Now here's a pen . . .' he said, flinging over a chewed-up Bic. 'Get to work.'

'Doing what?' I said.

'Signing 'em, of course.'

'But I don't need to cash them.'

'You're not cashing them, Yank,' Les said. 'You're signing 'em over.'

'To whom?'

'Us.'

'You are joking.'

'No, we are not,' Les said.

'But . . . but . . . it's *my* money.'

'Not any more. There's no such thing as personal assets in Wollanup. Nobody has money of their own. Nobody carries money. And anybody who comes to live in this community must donate all capital and possessions with him to the town coffers. So your van is now ours. And your money is now ours . . . but, hey, we'll let you keep your clothes.'

'I won't sign.'

'Oh, you will,' Les said.

'No. Fuck you. No.'

My voice quivered as I spoke. There was a huge, startled silence. Then the Town Council of Wollanup burst into amused hee-haws.

'Balls like Niagara Falls, this bloke,' Daddy said before clipping my nose with the tips of his fingers. Though he barely touched it, his aim was brutally deft – catching the damaged cartilage with just enough force to make it seem as if a nail had been hammered into the front of my face. As I yelped, Daddy crouched down beside me and spoke in a mild mannered, perfectly rational manner.

'I really would advise you to sign them cheques. 'Cause, y'see, your current position could best be described as *no-win*. If you refuse, we will cause you pain. More pain than you have ever experienced in your life. If you still remain stupid, then we will have to get real nasty and crush both your kneecaps. Or get Gus here to slice up your Achilles' tendon. And after going through all that, the joke will be on you –

because you'll *still* end up signing over the cheques.' He held up the pen in front of me. 'So, son-in-law – don't you think you should take the easy way out?'

Sixty-five hundred dollars. I used to save a hundred bucks a month back in the States – because after taxes and little things like rent and food, that's all I could afford to put aside on a journalist's salary. Sixty-five hundred dollars – five and a half years of economizing. My entire net worth. Destitute without it . . . but dead with it.

I snatched the pen from Daddy's fat fingers and signed. When I finished, I pushed the pile to the far-edge of the desk and turned away. I couldn't bear to watch Les going through every cheque, making sure I had endorsed them all. Then he tossed my stripped assets back into the safe, shut it with a jail-like clang, and gave me a cordial slap on the back.

'Good on ya, mate,' he said, full of false *bonhomie*. 'Think we owe the Yank a beer after all that, don't you?'

'Think we got a town meeting to be getting on with,' Daddy said, and left the room. He was followed dutifully by Robbo and Les. When they were down the stairs, Gus turned to me and said, 'That was smart, mate. Believe me, you really did the right thing. The *mellow* thing.'

I stared at him hard.

'This is your idea of mellow?' I said.

'It'll get easier.'

'No, it won't.'

'You'll adjust.'

'Bullshit.'

'You will – because you *have* to. You've got no choice. And Daddy –'

'What's with this "Daddy" crap?' I interrupted. 'The guy's got a real name, doesn't he?'

'Yeah . . . and it's *Daddy*.'

'Why – because he's your equivalent of Jim Jones or Charlie-fucking-Manson?'

'Careful, mate. Be real careful.'

103

Robbo came to the foot of the stairs and shouted up to us. 'Daddy wants the Yank down here now.'

'What Daddy wants,' Gus said, leading me out, 'Daddy gets.' He tightened his grip on my elbow. 'One final piece of advice: watch that lip of yours . . . if you don't want to be separated from it.'

Downstairs, they were waiting for me. The entire population of Wollanup. All fifty-three of them. Clustered around four tables. Four tables, four groups, four families. With the exception of the heads of those families and their wives, no one in the room was older than twenty-five – and at least half the population were still in single digits. It was easy to identify Gus's brood – his wife and eight children all looked like some unwashed Californicated clan who had just crawled out of a cave marked 'Alternative Living.' Robbo and Les both had ten brats each – their wives Sumo-like in shape, and all the kids travelling down a similar road towards serious pudge-dom.

And then there was my family.

'Hey darl,' Angie said, throwing her arms around my neck, then giving me this big wet public kiss. I smiled – like the Ecstatic Newlywed she wanted me to be.

'Daddy said the two of you just hit it off beaut.'

'Real beaut,' I said.

She turned to her siblings and said, 'Well, here he is! And isn't he looking a little better than when you last saw him?'

'Should've kept him in that chicken coop,' Daddy muttered before stepping behind the bar.

'You're a giggle, Daddy.'

'What happened to his nose and eye?' asked a brittle little woman well past forty – her brillo-like blonde hair streaked with grey, a roll-up ciggie parked in the right corner of her mouth.

'Love bite,' Angie said, adding, 'Darl, meet my mum, Gladys.'

'Nice to meet you, ma'am,' I said, extending my hand. She didn't take it.

'Landed yourself in something sweet, haven't you, Yank?'

'Mum, please . . .' Angie said.

'Please what? Look at this dillpot. Told you to pick no foreigner. Told you to find some Ocker, some dumb bushie who'd fit in here. But what d'you come back with? A useless Yank-wank.'

'Not useless to me,' Angie said, getting petulant.

'You never bloody listen to sense, girl,' Gladys said.

'You never bloody *talk* sense.'

'Little Miss Know-It-All. Daddy's little Princess . . .'

'Daddy . . .' Angie whined.

'Yeah, right, enough,' Daddy said. 'Finish the introductions and let's get this meeting started.'

Angie, still seething, reeled off the names of her siblings. The youngest was a three-year-old named Sandy, followed by four other girls of various ages, then twin eighteen-year-old boys, Tom and Rock, who acknowledged me with sullen nods. And finally there was the eldest child, Krystal. Twenty-three. Straw-blonde hair. Tall and big-shouldered, but not possessing Angie's robust bulk or her dangerous affability. Her features lacked the sun-cracked hardness which characterized most Wollanup faces. There was something almost genteel about her demeanour. Her green eyes were big and wide and troubled. She didn't belong here.

'Krystal's the brains of the family,' Angie said. 'Real smart. Ain't that right, teach?'

'You're a teacher?' I said.

She avoided my eye, choosing a spot on the lino to stare at while talking to me. 'I run the local school, yes,' she said.

'You and . . .?'

'No one. I'm the only teacher in town.'

'That's 'cause everyone else is so stupid here,' Angie shouted, much to the amusement of all the kids in the bar.

'My sister was telling me you're a reporter.'

'Used to be.'

'Maybe you can come talk to the children about journalism

one day. Tell them about the States and how newspapers work and –'

'Nah,' Daddy barked. 'The Yank is working with me in the garage.'

'But, surely, Daddy,' Krystal said, 'you could let him come over to the school for an hour one day –'

'He works in the garage. Period.'

There was an awkward silence, then Krystal nervously shrugged her shoulders. 'Sorry,' she whispered to me.

'That's all right,' I said. And, taking a chance, I added in a low voice, 'By the way, I was sad to hear about your husband.'

For a moment, she looked as if I had slapped her across the face. But she quickly composed herself, acknowledged my condolences with a dignified 'Thank you' and returned to her seat.

'Right,' Daddy said. 'This town meeting's in session. Who wants to start things off?'

The heads of the four families were perched on stools in front of the bar – like judges in some Supreme Kangaroo Court. Which is actually what the town meeting turned out to be – a forum to air grievances, to argue for better civic conditions, to demand justice, or plead for mercy. Local government at its finest – as long as you accepted the *l'état, c'est nous* mentality of Daddy and his three stooges.

One of Angie's twin brothers, Rock, had the first complaint.

'I'm like real sick of nothing but pineapple and prunes for sweets. They're, y'know, fart fodder. And I think I speak for a lot of the kids here when I say that we'd like some proper sweets in the shop. Chockie and stuff.'

Les – wearing his grocer's hat – fielded this question, saying that buying decent chocolates in bulk was far too expensive, but he'd try to increase the supply of cooking chocolate he kept in the general store.

'But that chockie is crappo,' Rock said.

'Too bloody bad,' Les said. 'It's all we can get.'

One of Robbo's teenage daughters asked if, at least, he

might consider stocking another type of tinned fruit – for the sake of variety.

'Think the supplier might have some pitted cherries. Talk to him on my next provision run.'

'They nice, cherries?' the kid asked.

'Yeah, great,' Les assured her – and it suddenly struck me that, growing up in Wollanup, you might just think that there are only two types of fruit in the world . . . and they both grow in cans.

Grievances about supplies dominated the meeting. Gladys complained about two packs of stale cigarette tobacco sold to her last week and made what I learned later was her weekly plea for proper brand-name smokes (a plea which Les always ignored). Robbo's eldest son, Greg, said that the razor blade ration should be increased to one per week, while his wife Carey spoke out for larger-sized sanitary towels – a demand which caused titters among every child in the room until Daddy silenced them by growling, 'Shaddup'.

Listening to these shopping requests made me understand just what a powerful role Les played in the life of the community. He was their conduit to the outside world – the man who decided what they could or could not consume. And I made a quick mental note to find out a.s.a.p. how and when he made these 'provision runs'.

'Any other business?' Daddy asked.

Gus announced that the bonfire barbie would take place as scheduled on the last Saturday of this month – and would everybody please make a civic effort to get all spare kangaroo heads off the road and on to the garbage mountain before sundown on the day. And then Robbo reminded everyone that the annual dog cull would take place two weeks before-hand – which meant that it was every family's obligation to put down five mutts that day, in order to keep the Wollanup canine population under control.

'And I don't want to see no dog bodies out on the road like

last year,' Robbo said. 'They go straight on the mountain, understand?'

'Okay,' Daddy said. 'I want Charlie and Lea up here. Now.'

Two pimply kids – they couldn't have been more than sixteen – stood up and walked to the bar, nervously exchanging glances with each other.

'You didn't think we knew?' Daddy said, his voice calm. 'You didn't think we'd find out, did you?'

Lea began to whimper. Charlie immediately took her hand.

'You let go of her right now,' Daddy shouted. Lea sobbed loudly; Charlie's knees appeared to be on the verge of buckling.

'Robbo, Mavis,' Daddy said, 'He's your boy. What you think we should do here?'

'Teach him a lesson,' Robbo said. 'Teach him good.'

'Tom, Rock – get up here and hold him,' Daddy said.

His two sons grabbed each of Charlie's arms. Daddy stood up, cracked his knuckles and – before getting down to business – turned to us and said, 'Watch and watch good. This is what happens to shit-wits who break the rules.'

He then spun around and, with one flowing circular motion, landed his right fist against Charlie's cheekbone. It was a terrifying punch. Nothing was held back, Daddy using the full weight of his body to generate maximum force, maximum damage. Lea screamed loudly, but to no avail, as Daddy – after pausing to catch his breath – wound up and landed another Exocet jab on Charlie's face. And another. And another. And another.

Angie, sitting by my side, took my hand and squeezed it hard. I could watch no more and turned away to find Krystal's eyes locked on to me like radar. But as soon as I met her gaze, she turned away, white-faced. Meanwhile, the blows continued to hammer down.

Four punches later, Daddy finally tired. 'Take him out, clean him up,' he ordered his sons – though it was pretty obvious that, after the pounding he took, it would take months for Charlie to get properly cleaned up.

As Tom and Rock dragged him out – followed in hot pursuit by Charlie's mom – Daddy took a swig or two of his beer and regained his composure.

'So,' he said, back to his easy-going self, 'any final public announcements before we call it a night?'

Angie's hand suddenly shot up.

'Yes, Princess?' Daddy said, all smiles for his little girl.

'I've got some news,' she said, a coquettish beam crossing her lips. 'Some real big news.'

'Spill it,' Daddy said.

'I'm pregnant.'

six

'Y ou lied to me,' I said.

'Can you believe my bloody mum?' she said.

'You said it was safe.'

'Always telling me off like that, always getting on my tits . . .'

'You said there was nothing to worry about.'

'A total cow, that's what she is. One big total fucking cow . . .'

'You didn't level with me.'

' 'Course, she'll have to start treating me nice, now that I'm preggers . . .'

'Deliberate goddamn deception, that's what this is. Do you know what you've done . . . what you've gotten us into?'

I was shouting. She was smiling.

'Yeah, I know.'

'You tricked me.'

'You tricked yourself.'

'If I'd known it wasn't safe, I would have taken precautions . . .'

'I didn't say it was, like, totally one hundred per cent safe. I just said "no worries". *You* decided to take the risk. And anyway, you only asked me if I was using something after you'd poked me a few times.'

'Then why'd you tell me you'd had your period while I was in the chicken coop?'

'Guess I didn't want to spoil our honeymoon.'

'It was a fucking lie, Angie . . .'

Another naïve little-girl grin.

' 'Spose it was.'

'Jesus . . .'

'No use going mental, Nick-o. Because there's nothing you can do about it. Anyway . . .' She shoved me on the bed, then straddled my ribcage with her knees until it hurt. '. . . . aren't you pleased?'

It wasn't a question; it was a threat.

'Delighted.'

'I'm so glad,' she said rolling off me. 'The way you were talking I thought you weren't happy about the news.'

'Just . . . surprised, that's all.'

'What d'you think of Sonny for a boy and Cher for a girl?'

I think I am going to work very hard at being twelve thousand miles away when this kid arrives, that's what I think.

'Great names,' I said.

'Daddy looked so pleased, didn't he? First grandchild and all that.'

Daddy actually used the occasion to get drunk. Dead drunk. As soon as Angie made her little shock announcement, he ordered that the bar be thrown open in celebration and proceeded to pour half a case of lager down his gullet in around thirty minutes. Once sloshed, he succumbed to Neanderthal sentimentality, throwing his arms around Robbo and Les (also awash in beer) and getting all heartfelt. 'Me Princess's gonna be a mum,' he half-bawled into Robbo's ear. 'Hear that, y'bastard? Little Angie a mum . . .'

His wife was not enjoying the party, let alone his mawkishness. 'Give it a fucking rest, eh?' she snapped at him – and he shut up on the spot, meekly backtracking to the bar in search of another beer. Then Gladys turned her tongue on me.

'Congrats, Yank,' she said, relighting the cigarette in the corner of her mouth. 'You've made that lughead a happy man. For the moment, anyway.'

'You're not pleased?' I asked.

'Not particularly. Are *you*?'

'Well . . . sure.'

' 'Course you're bloody not. It's written all over you. Bet you didn't even know she was up the spout.'

'It was, uh, something of a . . .'

'Fucking bombshell?' she said, finishing my sentence.

'You could say that.'

'Bet I could. Well, here's another bombshell for you. All those plans you've got in your puny brain about escaping from here – and, believe me, I know you're thinking them – piece of advice: just forget 'em. Because now that you've got Daddy's little "Princess" knocked up, he really will kill you if you try to run. Kill you and relish the job.' She shot me a spiteful smile. 'Enjoy the party, Yank.'

As Gladys drifted off in a cloud of cigarette smoke, an arm locked around my neck and began to goad my Adam's apple towards my vertebrae. When I tried fighting against this stranglehold, I was rewarded with a big wet drunken kiss on the forehead. Daddy was being alarmingly affectionate.

'Could fucking break your neck, I could,' he said, tightening his grip. 'Could break it like a twig. But then there'd be no daddy for my grandchild, right?'

'Right.'

'Little baby got t'have a daddy, y'know.'

'I know.'

He decided to stop garrotting me, but still kept his arm tightly around my shoulder. 'You're gonna be good daddy, yeah?'

'I promise.'

'And you're gonna keep Princess real happy, unnerstand?'

'I do.'

'You be good hubby, good daddy, y'do okay here.'

'I'll be very good.'

'Hold ya t'that, y'bastard.' He then proceeded to do that very Angie thing of emptying a can of beer over my head. 'Never thought I'd have a Yank for a son-in-law. But y'orright. Least I think y'orright. But rem'mber – your' neck's a fucking twig if y'stop being orright. And y'better be at the garage six tomorrow morning, ready t'start work . . .'

He staggered off back to the bar, calling out for another can of piss to replace the one he'd used for my baptism. As I scanned the room for Angie, I was hit in the head by a flying hand-towel.

'Dry yourself off,' Krystal said.

'Thanks,' I said, mopping up my beer-drenched hair.

'Daddy's dangerous when he's had a few.'

'Daddy strikes me as dangerous every waking moment of the day.'

'He is,' she said, avoiding my gaze. 'You must be careful.'

'I've been set-up.'

'I know.'

'Like your husband, right? Wasn't he set-up too?'

She turned white again – and I regretted asking the question.

'Must go,' she said, and bolted across the room and out the door before I had the chance to say anything more. Then I felt a hand goose my rump.

'Chatting up my sister, eh?'

It was Angie. Loaded.

'Just talking.'

'Ran off bloody fast. Whatcha say to her?'

'That you gave great head.'

'Good on ya,' Angie laughed, her face landing on my shoulder.

'Time to get you home,' I said, trying to hold her up.

'Need 'nother beer,' she said.

'You're blotto.'

'Drinking for two,' she said, and then succumbed to a fit of the giggles. I seized her tightly by the arm and frogmarched her to the door.

'Say nighty-night.'

'Nighty-night,' she shouted to her family.

Not a word was spoken between us until we got back to our hovel, whereupon she sobered up and we had that little exchange about the rhythm method of contraception . . . after which she tried to break my ribs with her knees.

Sonny and Cher. As I lay in bed that night – Angie's arms engulfing me like octopus tentacles – those names kept reverberating in my head. I never wanted marriage, and I certainly never wanted kids. Never felt the need to replicate my miserable self. But now I was going to be a daddy to . . .

Sonny and Cher . . . Sonny and Cher . . . Sonny and Cher.

It sounded like a death knell.

I shuddered and blanked out the thought with sleep.

I woke to the sound of retching. Angie was in the latrine, hugging the porcelain, suffering divine retribution for all that beer she'd swilled the night before. Though when she finally spoke, her first words were: 'Bloody morning sickness.'

The nasty bastard in me enjoyed her agony, considering it proper recompense for all the gastro-intestinal fun I had suffered in the chicken coop. And when she was eventually hit with a bout of the dry heaves, I put on my best concerned husband voice and said, 'Feeling bad, dear?'

'Real crook.'

'Maybe you should lie down.'

'Can't,' she said, as another swell of nausea overcame her.

'Think you can face the meat factory today?' (I really was enjoying this).

'No way.'

'Can of beer might help . . .'

'Uhhhhhhhhhhhhhhhhhh,' she gagged, her face turning a nice shade of puce.

'Maybe I should tell Robbo you need the day off.'

'Please . . .'

I threw on a T-shirt and an old swimsuit – work clothes. Then I gave Angie another happy hubby smile.

'Bye-bye dear. Have a *nice* day.'

It was a few minutes before six and, despite the thin dawn light, the Wollanup working day had already begun. As I walked the quarter-mile into town, I could hear the singsong voices of children in the schoolhouse. They were belting out an old nursery rhyme:

> *'Mary had a little lamb*
> *Its fleece was white as snow*
> *And everywhere that Mary went*
> *Her lamb was sure to go.*
> *It followed her to school one day*
> *That was against the rules . . .'*

The closer I got to the school, the clearer I could hear Krystal's voice rising above the din. When I reached this open-air shed, I paused on the opposite side of the road to watch her lead her ten pupils through the singsong chorus. She was standing at the front of the class, dressed in a simple white cotton shift, a pair of old hornrimmed glasses balanced on the tip of her nose. Very schoolmarmish. Curiously fetching. But when she looked up from her nursery primer and caught sight of me, her eyes snapped back down to the printed page. I took this as a cue to move on.

> *'. . . It made the children laugh and play*
> *To see a lamb at school.*
> *And so the teacher turned it out,*

The Dead Heart

But still it lingered near,
And waited patiently about
Till Mary did appear.'

Hats off to the planning genius who decided to situate an abattoir next to a schoolhouse. Wollanup Meats was a thirty-second stroll from the open-air classroom, and the grinding crank of its machinery threatened to drown out Mary's Little Lamb. And, in case any of Krystal's charges got bored with nursery rhymes, they could always glance sideways and catch the delightful spectacle I was currently witnessing – as a flat-bed truck pulled up in front of the warehouse, piled high with freshly shot kangaroos. My two brothers-in-law, Tom and Rock, climbed out of the cab and into the open back of the vehicle. Then, standing knee-deep in dead 'roos, they began to toss the carcasses out on to the concrete forecourt of the meat plant. Robbo – wearing hip-hugging wellies and a blood-splashed plastic apron – gave each beast a cursory inspection with the toe of his boot before two of his assistants dragged it inside. Another pair of workers immediately relieved them of the cadaver, fastening a metal clamp around its hind-legs. The clamp was attached to a thick wire, which then winched the animal up to a conveyor-belt. It travelled upside down for a few yards before stopping above a large plastic vat where Gladys was waiting, armed with a machete. She was wearing what appeared to be a body-sized plastic garbage bag, a white shower-cap and ski goggles. While puffing away on the ciga-rette between her teeth, she grabbed the 'roo's ears in one hand, jerked them down, then slashed its jugular vein with the cane-cutter. There was an initial geyser-like spurt of blood, followed by a steady downpour into the vat. When Gladys was satisfied that the creature's circulatory system was empty, she pressed a button and the animal wended its way to an adjoining vat, where a guy with an electric chainsaw decap-itated it. Once headless, it moved on to a third vat, where one of Robbo's teenage daughters used a scalpel to cut a circular incision around the roo's midsection. Then, ripping back the flesh with both hands, she reached inside the stomach cavity and yanked out all the entrails, cutting away at any stubborn bits of intestine or bowel that refused to come loose.

'Beaut work, Mags,' Robbo called out to his daughter. Then, catching sight of me standing opposite the plant, he said, 'Where's your bloody missus?'

'Sick?' I said.

'All that piss she was throwing back last night, I ain't surprised.'

'She's calling it morning sickness.'

'Yeah, right. Lucky for me that Mags stood in for Angie while she was off travelling.'

'That's Angie's job?' I said, watching Mags disembowel a newly beheaded 'roo.

'A real artist with a knife, your boss. Empties 'em out in thirty seconds flat – and never a trace of leftover gut in the thorax. When it comes to anatomy, Angie's just ace. Y'see, we don't just sell 'roo meat, we also make some dosh out of the heart, the liver *and* the entrails. Which means that she's gotta cut 'em out real delicate, 'cause the pet food company will only take intact internal organs. Used to be Gladys's job, but . . .' He lowered his voice into confidential octaves. '. . . to tell the truth, she was too bloody savage when it came to knowing where to cut. Gladys, y'see, is a bruiser – which is why she's much better off dealing with the jugular. But Angie . . . now there's a lady with real finesse. Though y'better warn her that if she starts missing work like this, Mags might just grab her place.'

My wife, the artist. The best disemboweller in Wollanup. What an honour.

'You seem to have quite a little operation here,' I said, trying my best to avoid breathing too deeply. My nostrils weren't accustomed to the scent of steamy entrails.

'Can get through sixty 'roos before we close down at noon.'

'Why just work the morning?'

'Only a shit-for-brains would want to be dealing with meat in the afternoon heat.'

'Where d'you get the meat?'

'Big open bush on the ridge above the town. Come sundown, it turns into a 'roo social club – which is when Tom and Rock go in with guns blazing.'

'Only Tom and Rock go hunting?'

He immediately knew what I was thinking and narrowed his eyes. 'No one else is allowed up that hill.'

'Yourself, Gus, Les and Daddy excluded, of course.'

'You got it.' His right paw encircled my arm, squeezing it hard. 'Lemme show you the rest of the operation,' he said, hauling me into the main production area. 'Now, after we've gutted the 'roos, we give 'em a little bath.' The 'bath' was actually another vat, filled with boiling water. 'We call this the scalding pot', Robbo said. 'Drop 'em in for sixty seconds, you can peel the fur right off 'em. Nasty punishment, ain't it?' He showed me the two teeth still left in his mouth – his idea of a grin.

'I better get to work,' I said, managing to shake my arm free of his grip.

'Yeah,' he said. 'You better.'

I had to stop myself from running out of the plant. When I reached the road, the garbage mountain suddenly smelled Alpine fresh.

Daddy's garage was down a dirt track behind the warehouse. It was nothing but a shed, surrounded by a junk heap of half-corroded fenders and car doors and bucket seats and exhaust pipes and smashed-up windscreens. The only intact vehicle was a large elderly refrigerator truck, the name 'Wollanup Meats' painted in a shaky hand on both side panels. As I approached the vehicle, Daddy shot out from under it, lying face up on a mechanic's roller-board. Oil had leaked all over him. He could have passed for Al Jolson.

'You're late,' he said.

'Angie was unwell.'

'Work begins at six sharp, no later. Got me?'

'Sorry.'

'Go to the shed – got a job for you there.'

I walked over to this wooden hut and swung open the door. There stood my Volkswagen microbus. A reassuring sight – until I saw that the van was on blocks, the hood open, and every component of the engine spread out across the clay floor. Like one of Robbo's dead 'roos, it had been totally gutted. I stared at it dumbly – a giant picture-puzzle, now fractured into a thousand little pieces. I turned away and found Daddy standing at the door, his blackened face aglow in the sun.

'Well, don't just stand there,' he said. 'Put it all back together again.'

seven

A week's work earned me 40 chits. The Wollanup minimum wage. Enough to fill my belly with food, my lungs with smoke, and to fog my brain every night with beer.

The *chit* was the local makeshift currency.

Makeshift really was the operative word here, because it was nothing more than an old-style Admit One ticket – the kind of stub used by travelling circuses or provincial picture shows. Les had dozens of rolls of these tickets under heavy guard in the Wollanup Central Bank (his safe). Every Friday, the entire working population of the town would line up in front of the pub to receive their weekly reward for thirty-five hours of toil . . . and come away with an elongated strip of movie tickets. The colour of these tickets changed every week – because the currency was only good for one seven-day period.

'We don't like the idea of savings,' Gus explained to me one night in the pub. 'Leads to people hoarding their dosh and getting competitive with each other and saying stuff like "you got more than me". So that's why we decided that, what you earn in a week, you have to spend in a week. Keeps everybody on the same level and cuts out all sorts of aggro.'

I have to admit that the chit system was surprisingly clever when it came to meeting your individual needs. It was predicated on two basic givens about the Wollanup citizenry – everybody over the age of fourteen drank and smoked. Which meant that, first and foremost, the alcohol and tobacco needs of the working populace had to be met.

'The way we figured it,' Gus said, 'most of us guzzle around twelve tinnies a day and get through four packs of cigarette tobacco a week. So we constructed the wage system to guarantee that nobody was ever parched or screaming for a smoke.'

A six-pack of beer cost 1 chit; a pack of tobacco, 2 chits – a weekly total of 22 chits, if you stuck to the prescribed twelve cans a day/four packs a week diet. Which left you with 18 chits to budget out like this:

4 lbs kangaroo meat:	2 chits
4 cans tinned meat:	4 chits
8 cans tinned vegetables:	2 chits
1 lb powdered milk:	1 chit
8 oz powdered eggs:	2 chits
24 oz instant coffee:	3 chits
2 rolls toilet paper:	½ chit
1 box washing powder:	½ chit
7 bars chocolate:	3 chits
1 lb sugar:	2 chits
Chewing gum:	1 chit

Of course, these remaining 18 chits were not enough to run a household, so every family received a further 10 chits per child. Schoolchildren were given 5 chits a week for pocket money. When they joined the workforce at the age of fourteen, they were only paid 30 chits for their first four years of employment – in order to restrict their beer intake to a mere six-pack a day.

Along with our streamer of chits, everyone in town was also given a weekly toiletries pack – a paper bag with a small cake of soap and a tube of toothpaste. Luxury items like shampoo, deodorant, shaving cream or talcum powder were not available in Wollanup. A free toothbrush was supplied to everyone once a month, a disposable razor every other week, and one-size sanitary towels were available on demand for women. If you needed medical supplies, you had to tango with Gus, who acted as the town's stop-gap medicine man. An alcove in his home had been turned into an improvized pharmacy and emergency room, and he told me with great pride that he'd once performed a successful appendectomy on his kitchen table.

'Didn't know you'd trained as a doctor,' I said.

'Yeah,' he said, 'Six months in a Perth med school.'

In addition to this ad-lib national health service, Wollanup residents were also entitled to free clothing – but only on the basis of absolute need. Les kept a stash of cheap T-shirts and shorts and socks and underpants in the back of his shop, but to qualify for a new garment you had to hand over an old one that was in an irredeemable state of decay. A small tear in your knickers wouldn't entitle you to a new pair – the crotch had to be decomposing before Les would deem them worthy of exchange. And when I first visited his general store, he scrutinized my brand-name shorts and T-shirt and said, 'Looks like I won't have to outfit you for around five years.'

Five years. Late at night, I would often snap awake. To the accompaniment of Angie's metronomic snores, I would stare at the tin ceiling and think: *Life without parole in Wollanup.* Was this really my final destiny? Like any prisoner sentenced to eternal incarceration, I had to hope against hope that, one bright morning, someone in authority would slap me on the back and say, 'The joke's over – you can go now'. Or that there was a way out of this maximum security lockup.

I knew, of course, that everybody was just waiting for me to attempt an escape – which is why I decided to think strategically for the first time in my life and do nothing dramatic for my first couple of weeks in town. Especially since there was no conventional way of breaking out – no fences to scale or barbed wire to cut or tunnels to crawl through. Just that one damn rocky road – a steep climb to nowhere. I estimated it would take around four hours to hike to the plains above Wollanup. But even if I got there undetected, then what? A 700k walk to the next town? Down an unsealed road in hundred degree heat? No thanks. Best to suppress all my convoluted feelings of despair and fear and anger, and instead pretend that I was adjusting to my new lot in life – while sussing out chinks in the Wollanup fortifications.

So I threw myself into the reconstruction of my van's engine – arriving at the garage every morning at five, working long beyond the High Noon knockoff hour. I didn't simply want to get the engine operative again, I was determined to rebuild it entirely, to transform it into a masterpiece of internal combustion and prove my mechanical worth to that fat shit Daddy.

The job took almost three weeks. It was an insane labour of love. Every component of the engine was cleaned and overhauled, using whatever spare parts I could find in Daddy's garage. I decoked and polished the valves. Decoked the cylinder head. Renewed the valve springs. Installed new piston rings and new bearings and a good set of plugs. Fitted a new carburettor. Rebalanced the crank shaft. Replaced the starter motor. Serviced the rotor arm in the distributor. Renovated all wiring. Overhauled the hot-rod exhaust. And then – as a final flourish – I hand-scrubbed the engine block until it shined like a Marine's dress-boots.

I loved the work – because it occupied the day, killed time, gave me a reason to get up in the morning. We go through life pretending that our toil has a higher purpose – something beyond the material means to keep ourselves housed, clothed, fed. But, in the end, we really work to fill the hours – to avoid confronting the meagre significance of our lives. Stay busy, stay stressed and you don't have to reflect on the abject futility of your time on the planet. Or the cul-de-sac you've landed in. A cul-de-sac that you've inevitably created for yourself.

So I put in ten-hour days and became obsessed with the minutiae of the task at hand – fretting over the special needles that powered the carburettor, calculating the right amount of oil needed to grease the bearings. Like a beleaguered suburbanite, I allowed workaholism to subsume all thoughts of domestic entrapment. And I discovered that occupational exhaustion also functioned as an effective Novocaine against the dull ache of home life. Up at five-thirty, home with the crippling afternoon heat at three-thirty, I made sure I was covered from head to toe in engine lubricants, thereby forestalling Angie's immediate physical advances. By the time I emerged from the shower and began to down the first of six beers I'd drink before dinner, Angie was usually snoozed-out – her 'Preggers Nap', as she called it. When she snapped back awake at six, I had dinner under control – having managed to wrestle command of the kitchen away from my wife's toxic hands. After serving up a simple powdered-egg omelette or some heavily-seasoned, heavily-grilled cut of 'roo meat, we'd stroll back into town and while away the final two hours of the day at the pub. Then it was back home and in bed by nine.

Boredom: the great domestic disease. It was especially rife in Wollanup – a place lacking in such great time killers like television, shopping malls, bowling alleys, and Top 40 radio. Even reading material was hard to come by. Besides the basic primers used in Krystal's schoolhouse, the only books in town were a shelf of trashy paperbacks in Les's shop. Thirty-five airport novels to be exact (I counted them one day), which hardly anyone borrowed because reading took up too much drinking time. And drinking was the leading amusement of choice in Wollanup. Unless, like me, you also had an engine to work on.

As the microbus started to come together, I found myself wondering: might it be my salvation? Might it eventually deliver me from Wollanup? Once it was back in pristine shape, Les would surely want to use it on one of his provision runs to Kalgoorlie (since it would be in better running order than his own van). Couldn't I stow away? Maybe create a hollowed-out hiding place beneath one of the bunks and figure out a way to deposit myself there late one night before Les's pre-dawn departure.

I didn't have a definitive plan as yet. But as I started to create a small cavity beneath one of the bunk-beds, I was reacquainted with the notion of hope. Without hope, you can never get through the day. With it, you can even believe that you have a future beyond this death-within-life called Wollanup. And so I became even more obsessed with finishing the microbus — because I knew it was my one hope, my only conduit to my future.

'You really love that heap-of-shit van, don't you?' Angie said, one night in bed.

'Just want to get it right.'

'Love it more than me.'

'Of course I love you,' I lied, my instinct for survival overshadowing any impulse towards emotional honesty.

'But not as much as your Kraut-tank. You're almost living with the bloody thing.'

'I'm only trying to show Daddy that I know what I'm doing as a mechanic.'

That shut her up. And when I finally did unveil the reconstructed engine to Daddy, it actually shut him up too. For a moment, anyway.

It was a Friday morning. I'd been up all night, making final adjustments to the engine, hoping that nobody had snuck a peek at what I'd been up to behind closed doors for the past week. Around five, the job was done and I slumped down by my creation on the dirt floor of the garage, lit a smoke, popped a beer and was thwacked by that peculiar wave of elation/deflation which always attends the completion of a major project. An hour later, I heard Daddy's approaching footsteps. Scrambling to my feet, I turned the ignition key and threw open the garage doors – a dramatic flourish which had the desired effect.

He stopped dead in his tracks and said, 'Fuck me.'

Just as I expected, it was the white that hit him first – jet-white paint that had been waxed and buffed to a brilliant gloss. Three coats of white paint had been needed to cover the fatigued camouflage colour of the old bodywork, and I'd also used an entire pot of filler to repair assorted fender perforations. It wasn't exactly a showroom finish, this paint-job – but compared to the state of the van before, it still dazzled the eye. Especially as the hubcaps had been polished to a metallic sheen, the chrome trim restored, the seats washed free of their Outback grime, the dashboard waxed, the living area thoroughly scoured, the windscreens spotless, crystalline. Then there was the motor itself. The hood was up and every element of the gleaming engine block hummed away with flawless sonority – like an orchestra in perfect tune.

Daddy approached the vehicle with something approaching reverence – running his finger along the frosty glaze of the bodywork, staring at the immaculate 1300hp reconstruction job beneath the hood, listening long and hard to the lyrical cadences of an engine which never once missed a beat.

Finally, he said, 'All your own work?'

I just smiled.

'Ever do this sort of thing before?'

'Nothing so big – and it was my first time tackling body-work?'

'Bloody amazing,' he said. 'Didn't know you had it in you.'

'Nor did I. Feel like a spin?'

'Feel like a beer, actually. A couple of coldies to celebrate. Finally got us a real fucking mechanic round here.'

'Thanks, Daddy.'

He looked at me with what seemed to be new-found respect. And said, 'Good on ya, Yank.'

I'd never been in a pub at six-fifteen in the morning. Daddy had the key (Les being away on one of his provision runs) – and when I mentioned that I had spent all my beer chits for the week, he told me that the piss was on the house. By eight, we'd put away a six-pack apiece and were joined by Gus and Robbo (on a break from the meat plant). By nine, another three beers had trickled down my gullet – and my father-in-law insisted that we all march back to the garage, so his two associates could admire my achievement. By ten, we were back in the pub – Gus and Robbo singing my praises as we raided the beer-chest yet again and fell into a rambling session of blokey car-talk. By eleven, Les had arrived back in town – which meant that it was over to the garage for another show-off session with the van, followed by the inevitable return to the pub for yet another three beers. By noon, Daddy and I were best friends.

'Les, you're t'give the Yank here an extra twenty-chit bonus this week for his beaut work.'

'Much appreciated, Daddy,' I said.

'A fuckin' mechanic,' he said, for around the tenth time that morning, giving me a big pissy smile before finally staggering out. I was wasted, but exhilarated by my accomplishment, by the warm accolades from Daddy and his three fellow henchmen, and (more tellingly) by the fact that, for the first time since landing in Wollanup, I actually felt comfortable here. At ease in the lethargic, boozy *bonhomie* of the pub. An accepted part of the furniture. Temporarily oblivious to my inmate status. Skunk-drunk.

I was so stewed that trying to get up off the bar stool was a major strategic operation. Les – noticing my parlous state –

helped me up and deposited me on a narrow cot in a tiny
back room, where I collapsed into sleep for the first time in
thirty-six hours.

He kicked me awake again at five that afternoon.

'Better get home for your dins,' he said.

Hungover before sunset – a new experience . . . and one not
worth repeating. I wandered into the hellhole pub toilet,
deflated my bladder, stuck my head under the tap and ran for
the door. As I started to head home, I decided to make a quick
detour to the garage – for a private ego-inflating glance at my
automotive handiwork before bringing Angie back to see it
later that night.

But as I approached the shed I heard the whirr of a drill, the
clang of metal meeting metal. And when I pulled open the
doors, I saw . . . carnage.

The engine block dismembered.

The tyres slashed.

The exhaust riddled with holes.

A can of black paint dumped over the hood.

The fenders smashed in.

And Daddy – shirtless, sweating – using a drill to perforate
the carburettor.

I stood there and slipped into shock. Impotent, powerless
shock. When Daddy finally saw me, he stopped work and
dropped the drill at my feet.

'Put it all back together again,' he said.

All I could mutter was, 'Why?'

'Because you're a fuckin' mechanic. That's why.'

eight

The dog cull began that night. The streets were alive with the sound of yelping and buckshot, as every household dragged out their five dingiest mutts and blew them away. We didn't have any dogs, but I wished we'd had a gun. I would have used it. First on Daddy. Then on his goddamn daughter.

'Daddy said you know shit about cars.'

'He's full of shit.'

'Said you did a crap job on the van . . .'

'He tore it apart . . .'

' 'Cause it was a crap job.'

'No way.'

'Said the thing wouldn't even start . . .'

'It was *perfect*.'

'Said you didn't even know how to fit a spark plug.'

'Fuckin' liar . . .'

'Don't call him –'

'Total fuckin' liar and a fuckin' savage too. Like everyone in this fuckin' town –'

Thwack! A right to the jaw. Without thinking, I reciprocated with a hard backhand across her face. It threw her sideways and she hit the concrete sitting-room floor with her bare knees. Immediately, she screeched; immediately, I was thumped by guilt. But when I leaned over to help her up and beg forgiveness, she caught me with one of those perfectly placed punches in the gut which make you feel like you've just been disembowelled. It knocked the wind out of me . . . and all traces of guilt.

I took refuge on the bed and baffled my head with a pillow as Angie went into another of her extended rants. She howled, she bellowed, she let everybody in town know that I was the most useless man on earth. A coward who had struck a pregnant woman. A twerp. A shit. A loser.

I didn't care. Break my van, break me. That fucker Daddy knew what he was doing, all right. And since his little Princess was also determined to run me into the ground, my attitude now was: let them. Because my situation here was hopeless, terminal. They want a zombie, I'll give 'em a zombie.

So I took to the bed. And didn't get up. I refused to talk. I refused all solid foods. On the first night of this enervating spell, I wouldn't even budge to use the latrine, wetting the bed while Angie was asleep beside me. Her patience was already strained at this point by my silence, my near-catatonic state – so turning the mattress into a urine reservoir really made her snap. She called me gross, repulsive, a sicko. That's when I decided to relax my sphincter muscle and really give her something to scream about.

And scream she did. Hysterically. Before bolting for the door.

When she returned twenty minutes later, she came armed

with medical assistance – Gus. He carried a little black doctor's bag and didn't look exactly pleased to be making a
housecall at two in the morning. When he saw the state of the
mattress, he was (as I'd hoped) truly nauseated.

'Fuckin' Yank animal,' he said. 'He been doing this
often?'

'No bloody way.'

'Just asking.'

'You think I'd *live* with this? Suffer in silence? Tell you this
much, if he shits the bed again, I'm putting 'em down just like
a dog. Hear that, Yank-wank?'

I did, but maintained my lost-in-space guise: body rigid,
eyes frozen, voice silent.

'What's wrong with him?' Gus asked.

'You're the bloody quack. You tell me.'

He got out a little pocket flashlight and shined the beam in
my eyes. Then he stuck a stethoscope to my chest and
bounced a rubber mallet off my knees. 'Well, he's still alive.
And everything seems to be working properly. Probably a
seizure of some sort. Or a breakdown.'

'Or a put-on job.'

'You don't shit yourself if you're faking being starkers.
Unless you're a real gross bastard.'

'He is.'

'You blame him for being a bit troppo? I mean, the bloke's
not exactly here of his own free will. And after what Daddy
did to his van . . .'

'It was a bloody fiasco, that van –'

'You see it after the Yank got done with it?'

'Nah, but Daddy said it was crook.'

'It was *magic*, Angie. Total magic. Your Yank did an ace job –
which Daddy then trashed.'

'Bullshit.'

'You don't believe me, you talk to Les or Robbo.'

'Why would Daddy trash it?'

'Envy's my guess. Envy and too much amber. You know

Daddy – hates being shown up and gets kind of crazy when pissed.'

'Gonna tell him you said that.'

'Go right ahead. And you can also tell Robbo that you're gonna need a couple of days off work to nurse Nick-o.'

'I ain't no nurse.'

'You are now. Anyway, there's nothing to it. Keep him fed, get a bucket under him every time he needs to go to the bog, wipe his ass when he's done. Get you in training for when your nipper comes along.

'And while you're at it, put some cold meat on that swollen jaw of his. Looks like you gave him quite a punch.'

'He hit me too.'

'Yeah – but you did more damage.'

He left. As soon as he was out of earshot, Angie turned back to me and hissed, 'You like shit, you sleep in it.'

And sleep in it I did, because Angie crashed out on the beanbag, leaving me prostrate between the soiled sheets. That's when I knew that I wasn't simply feigning signs of a breakdown – that something had indeed snapped and I was now in the twilight zone. Believe me, had I been just faking it, I would have called off the game by now – because no charade was worth lying all night in a pool of your own waste. But even though I wanted to spring off the mattress and fling the dirty bedclothes in Angie's face, I had no energy for this task. All back-up supplies of will had been depleted. I felt drained, devitalized, benumbed. I couldn't move and I couldn't have cared less. I had reached the point of no return. I didn't care about anything any more.

It was, thankfully, a short night. Angie was up by five, looking bruised and careworn after her stint on the beanbag. And when she saw that I hadn't moved from the bed – was, in fact, still inert on that foul mattress – her guilt became palpable.

'Oh, Christ . . .' she muttered under her breath before shaking me hard and shouting my name in my ear several times, imploring me to snap out of it. But when I didn't respond, she threw on some clothes and ran out the door. Half an hour later, she was back with her brothers Tom and Rock. They were lugging a rundown double mattress with them.

'Cripes, what a mess,' Tom said, grimly eyeing the state of the bed. 'And smell that pong . . .'

'You let him sleep in that all night?' Rock said.

'Thought he was pulling a fastie,' Angie said.

'Real angel of mercy, our sis,' Rock said to Tom.

'Shaddup and help me get him into the shower.'

The two boys insisted on making assorted melodramatic noises as they hoisted me off the bed, then hectored Angie with comments like:

'Is this really your idea of a sexy bloke?'

And . . .

'D'you always have to clean his bum, Ang?'

And . . .

'Maybe you should ask Les if he's stocking big nappies for big Yanks.'

Boys will be boys – but Angie was not amused, and barked at her brothers to kill the wisecracks and get on with the bloody job. So they dragged me to the shower, lay me on my side in the middle of the stall, and blasted the water over me until all nasty evidence of my incontinence had been washed away.

They left me in the stall while they turned their attention to the bed, bundling the sheets into a pillowcase, hoisting off the soaked-through mattress and sliding its replacement on to the box spring.

'What d'you want us to do with this crap?' Tom asked.

'Garbage mountain, of course.'

'Gonna cost you six beer chits,' Rock said.

'Real generous arseholes, aren't you?' Angie said.

'It's a grot job, sis,' Tom said.

'Six chits is highway robbery.'

'Get 'em off Nick then,' Rock said. 'Didn't he get paid before going mental?'

'Good point,' Angie said, and immediately started rifling through a pile of my clothes by the bed until she found two streamers of chits in the back pocket of my work shorts.

'Looks like you're gonna be able to double your piss intake this week,' Rock said.

'Not if I'm stuck here babysitting this log of wood. Y'wouldn't pick me up a case of tinnies at the shop, would you?'

'Cost you four more chits,' Tom said.

'Get fucked.'

'Two chits?'

'Done,' she said, and handed over a foot-long length of Wollanup play money to Tom. Then she ordered her brothers to lift me out of the shower and keep me standing while she towelled me dry. After managing to slip a T-shirt over my head, she had them drag me to the latrine and prop me up, butt-naked, on the toilet seat.

'You gonna leave him there?' Rock said, genuinely shocked.

'Well, I can't let him mess the bed again, now, can I? Especially since this is the only spare mattress in town.'

'Yeah, but . . . it's kind of cruel, isn't it?'

'Then you sit here and shove a pan under him every time he needs to take a squat.'

'No thanks,' Rock said.

'Bet you anything,' Angie said, 'that after a couple of hours sitting on the pot, he snaps out of his little dum-dum routine and starts acting sub-normal again.'

'You are one hard bitch,' Tom said.

'The hardest,' she shot back.

But she was right about one thing: after around three hours of sitting half-naked in that godawful latrine, my muddled brain did decide that enough was enough, and convinced me to rise up and shuffle back to bed. And as I climbed on to the 'new' mattress (still mushy, still sagging in the middle), Angie said, 'The dead walk!'

I curled up into a protective foetal position and didn't respond.

'Still acting the ding-dong, eh?'

I was – because though my toilet confinement had gotten me on my feet again, it hadn't suddenly yanked me back into normalcy. And I still found myself unwilling to speak or eat.

'Well, if you don't want to talk, that's fine by me,' Angie said. 'But I'm warning you – I'll lock you in that boghouse the moment you pull another stunt like last night.'

I heeded her warning and was perfectly potty-trained for the duration of my infirmity. But outside of calls of nature, I remained wedded to the bed and only sat up to be spoon-fed Angie's thin vegetable broth (a teaspoon of tinned carrots and beans boiled in a mug of water). She did try me on more substantial foods, but even something as bland and insipid as powdered scrambled eggs made me gag. So Angie begrudgingly kept me alive with the broth – hating every moment of her nursing duties, swilling beer and blaring her show tunes in an attempt to fill the hush of the house.

After three days, we'd gotten to the stage where she regarded me with the waspish dispassion of a geriatric nurse. I was the lump on the bed – to be given nourishment three times a day and otherwise ignored. She even stopped saying anything to me – merely tapping me on the shoulder to announce 'Tucker time!' then feeding me my broth with deep silent contempt.

On the second Saturday of my collapse, however, she finally did speak, tersely announcing that she was going to the pub tonight – because after a week indoors with me, she was ready for some serious drinking. And she was heading off now to find me a babysitter. She didn't return until dusk – and from her pissy demeanour when she staggered back through the door, I could tell that she had already been laying the groundwork for tomorrow's hangover.

'Little Baby happy t'see Mummy?' she asked, the words slurring. 'Little Baby didn't go poo-poo in the bed, did he?'

A voice behind her said, 'Leave the bloke alone, Angie.'

'Mummy brought Little Baby a playmate.'

Krystal walked in.

'Hey, Nick,' she said, trying to sound matter-of-fact. 'How's it going?'

'He won't bloody speak to you,' Angie said.

'Maybe he will.'

'Nah, he's turned into a spastic mute.'

Krystal was still willing to give it the old college try. And said, 'You've really lost a lot of weight, Nick.'

' 'Course he's lost weight,' Angie said. 'If you ate nothing but veggie soup for a week, you'd lose weight too.'

'I don't need to lose weight,' Krystal said, her eyes flickering over Angie's fleshy form.

'Cow,' Angie said.

'Any special instructions about looking after him?'

'There's some broth in the pan on the hot-plate. Just heat it up and feed him a mugful in about an hour. That's about it, really.'

'Away with you then,' Krystal said.

'You sure you don't mind?'

'I don't mind.'

'You're brill, Sis' – and she was gone out the door.

Krystal grabbed a kitchen chair and pulled it up by the bed.

' "Sleep with a crazy, you end up with a crazy" – I'd have thought an intelligent man like yourself would have known that that was rule number two of Outback life.'

A mischievous grin crossed her lips. An uncharacteristic grin – as it was the first time I had ever seen Krystal smile. Settling herself next to me, she spoke with an ease that had been absent whenever we'd previously met in public. 'You are going to talk to me, aren't you, Nick? Because there really is a lot to talk about.'

I managed a shrug of the shoulders.

'You take your time,' she said. 'Only speak when you're ready. But first . . . you need to eat. Especially since Angie's probably been feeding you swill.'

She crossed through the bead curtains to the kitchen area,

stuck a spoon into the pot of broth, took a small sip, and spat it out, her face contorted like someone who had accidentally sampled liquid sulphur.

'No wonder you've no appetite,' she said, dumping the pan in the sink. 'Let's see if I can do a little better.'

She rifled through the kitchen cabinets, appropriating assorted cans and seasonings. Half an hour later, she came back to the bed holding a steaming mug of broth.

'It's vegetable soup again, I'm afraid,' she said. 'Not much else I could do with the supplies on hand.'

She sat me up in bed and spoon-fed me the soup. Though it was the same mish-mash of carrots and beans, she had somehow managed to make it edible – and I scoffed the lot, accepting a second helping before dozing off. I stirred again when Angie came falling through the door. Krystal was still sitting next to me, a frayed school edition of *Robinson Crusoe* open on her lap.

'Ain't that a picture?' Angie said. 'Nursy-nurse keeps bed-side watch. He give you any trouble?'

'He's hardly moved all night.'

'Some sheilas have all the luck.' She belched. Loudly. 'Wouldn't want to babysit him again, would you?'

'I might,' Krystal said. 'For a price.'

'Eight chits?'

'Ten.'

'How 'bout eight for Wednesday night and ten for next Saturday – unless you're real keen to go to the garbage barbie.'

'I can miss it . . . for twelve chits.'

'Bitch.'

'Take it or leave it.'

Another big belch from Angie.

'You're on.'

As soon as Krystal left, the house went silent again for another seventy-two hours – and I found myself back on a diet of Angie's prison slop. By Tuesday, I was counting the hours until my sister-in-law returned.

'Is he any better?' Krystal asked when she finally arrived on Wednesday night, carrying a small string bag.

'Nah,' Angie said. 'Still acting the retard.'

But as soon as Angie was out the door, Krystal said, 'You are better, aren't you Nick?'

I didn't move.

'Better enough to eat an omelette, perhaps.'

I shook my head.

'Made with real eggs.'

I spoke my first words in nearly two weeks: 'Real eggs?'

Krystal welcomed me back to Planet Earth with a grin, then reached into her string bag and pulled out an egg-box. 'Half a dozen free-range,' she said. 'Bought yesterday by Les in Kalgoorlie. Along with a pound of cheddar and some button mushrooms. Think you could stomach that?'

'Could try.'

'Right, then – one cheese and mushroom omelette coming up. But while I'm cooking, how about you making a little visit to the shower? Because I'm not eating with a man who pongs. And at the moment, you really stink.'

She had a point – the last time I had made contact with running water was when Tom and Rock dragged me into the shower twelve days ago. And though I still felt physically drained, the exotic-for-Wollanup aroma of butter sizzling in a frying pan encouraged me to stagger into the shower.

As always, the water was wintry. But, after the initial shock, I appreciated the cold, and I now allowed it to rouse me out of the murk I'd been berthed in. I even dragged a razor across my face and worked slowly with the soap to rid myself of rankness. Then – as Krystal modestly averted her eyes – I tottered back to bed and threw on a pair of shorts.

'Feeling better?' she asked.

'A bit,' I said. But I suddenly went wobbly and had to stretch out again on the bed.

'Don't think you're ready for a sit-down meal yet,' Krystal said, coming over with two plates. 'Want me to feed you?'

'I'll manage.'

I took the plate and fork and was immediately overcome by the aroma of the omelette. After all that powdered and tinned produce, the scent of fresh food packed a punch. The fork shook a bit in my hand, but I managed to steady myself and spear a corner of the perfectly browned eggs. Then I bit into it and was back in Maine at the Miss Brunswick Diner: a truckstop off I-95 which served the best cheese and mushroom omelette I had ever encountered. Until now.

'It's okay?' she asked.

'Yeah,' I said. 'Very okay.'

'Eat it slowly. Your stomach needs to get used to solids again.'

I followed her command and worked my way carefully through it, valuing every bite. When I finished, Krystal reached into her bag and pulled out another surprise: a packet of Marlboros.

'Where d'you get them?' I said.

'Mooched them off of Les.'

'Didn't think he stocked real cigarettes . . . or fresh eggs.'

'Officially, he doesn't . . . but he still brings in a small selection of luxury foods every week for himself and his three cronies: frozen steaks and chickens, real eggs, good Australian wine, even the occasional bottle of top-class scotch. They don't share these goodies with their families – but instead keep them for their weekly get-together. Just the four of them in a room over the pub, chomping away on sirloins and filets and breasts of chickens, washing it all down with a nice Shiraz.

'Of course, they're incredibly secretive about the menu at these private feasts – because they know that with the rest of us existing on cuts of 'roo and Spam, there'd be hell to pay if anyone found out just how well they were eating.'

'Why does he share the stuff with you, then?'

'Guilt.'

'About what?'

'Jack.'

'Your husband?'

'We were never married.'

'But Angie said –'

'Angie's a liar . . . about a lot of things.'

I held up my left hand. 'This isn't his ring?'

'It's Jack's ring, all right. But it wasn't a wedding ring. Just some cheap thing he wore for fun.'

'Why is Les guilty about him?'

'Some other time, Nick.'

'They kill him?'

'Not now, please.'

'But –'

'*No.*'

She spoke with such vehemence that I immediately backed off.

'Sorry,' I said.

'That's all right,' she said, briefly squeezing my hand. 'You are going to smoke one of those Marlboros, aren't you?'

'Yeah, I'll smoke one.'

She handed me the pack and a box of matches. 'Can't let you keep them, I'm afraid. If Angie saw them, she'd tell our Mum, and she'd go berserk – 'cause you know Gladys and her campaign for name-brand ciggies. So it looks like you'll just have to get through as many as possible now.'

I broke open the pack and offered her one.

'I'm the only person over sixteen in Wollanup who doesn't smoke,' she said.

I fumbled with the matches, but managed to light one up, then drew a thick, aromatic cloud of smouldering Virginia tobacco into my lungs, shut my eyes, and exhaled.

'Thank you,' I said. 'Thank you very much. For everything.'

'What's it taste like, a Marlboro?'

I took another savoury drag.

'Home,' I finally said.

'Sorry to have made you homesick.'

'I'm homesick all the time.'

'Can't blame you. This is an awful place. Wasn't meant to be – but it really has turned out that way.' She burrowed through her bag again until she found a large battered manila envelope. 'Think you should have a look at this,' she said, handing it to me.

Inside were a small stack of newspaper clippings, yellowed and crumbly with age. The first was from the 12 March 1979 edition of the Perth *West Australian*.

THREE DIE IN ASBESTOS MINE BLAST
WOLLANUP, WA – Three miners died instantly yesterday when a botched dynamite charge rocked Union Minerals' asbestos mine in the Great Victoria Desert community of Wollanup. According to eyewitnesses, explosives had been placed deep within the mineshaft to assist in burrowing through some rock, but prematurely detonated, killing the three miners still on-site. They were Joe John Drysdale (55) and two brothers, Harold (51) and Buster (54) Reynolds, all married with children, all from Wollanup. Rescue workers have been unable to retrieve the bodies, as fires broke out in the mineshaft following the explosion.

'Buster Reynolds was my grandfather,' Krystal said. 'Daddy's daddy. And Harold was Les's father.'

I turned to the next clipping from the *West Australian*, date-marked 14 March 1979.

MINE BLAST TOWN TO BE EVACUATED
WOLLANUP, WA – The isolated mining community of Wollanup is to be evacuated, after an explosion in an asbestos mineshaft two days ago sparked fires which are still raging beneath the surface.

Announcing the evacuation from his office in Canberra, the Minister for Mines and Mineral

Resources, Mr Jock Smithson (Lib., Gold Fields), said: 'When an asbestos mine catches fire, the potential public health risk is huge. Three miners have already died in this tragic accident, we certainly don't want any further fatalities, so we have no choice but to order that the town be vacated immediately.' The 120 residents are to be driven 700k by coach to Kalgoorlie – the town nearest to Wollanup. Emergency accommodation will be provided by the WA Department of Social Services.

'I'll always remember that drive to Kalgoorlie,' Krystal said. 'I was ten at the time, and it was all incredibly traumatic. Daddy was in bits over his father's death, screaming how the mining company was to blame because they always used cut-priced explosives. Everyone else was crying about having to leave all their belongings behind. And it was the middle of summer, and the coaches they sent to get us weren't air-conditioned, and because of the bad roads it took over twenty hours to get to Kalgoorlie. When we finally arrived, they put us up in these godawful barracks on the outskirts of town. Army barracks which hadn't been used or cleaned in ten years and were full of rat droppings and blocked loos. Then, around three weeks later, the mining company which owned Wollanup stopped paying everybody's wages because they decided to close the town down.'

I reached for the subsequent clipping – 20 April 1979:

ASBESTOS MINE TO CEASE OPERATION
PERTH, WA – Union Minerals of Australia plc announced today that its asbestos mine in Wollanup – badly damaged in an explosion last month – will cease to operate, effective immediately. The company's senior vice-president for public affairs, Russell Hanley, said in a prepared statement: 'Union Minerals deeply regrets having to close an historic mine which has been in continuous operation since 1889. But the explosion and fires last month, in which three of our most senior employees

lost their lives, have rendered the mine permanently inoperable – especially as our safety experts inform us that asbestos fires are still smouldering beneath the surface.' The Union Minerals decision caused outrage among the Wollanup community, the majority of whom are still living in temporary accommodation in Kalgoorlie. The spokesmen for the Wollanup Action Committee – Millard and Lester Reynolds, who lost their father in the mine disaster told reporters, 'This means the death of our town.'

'Daddy's real name is *Millard*?' I said.

Krystal failed to suppress a giggle. 'Don't ever let on that you know. He really hates that name.'

'What happened after they closed the mine down?'

'It got ugly,' Krystal said. 'Very ugly.'

From the *West Australian*, 2 May 1979:

TWO ARRESTED IN MINE COMPANY DEMO

PERTH, WA – Violent clashes with police outside the corporate headquarters of Union Minerals in central Perth yesterday led to the arrest of two male protesters.

The two men – Millard and Lester Reynolds of the Wollanup Action Committee – were taken into police custody after assaulting Union Minerals spokesman Russell Hanley as he tried to leave the company's office block. Scuffles broke out when other protesters tried to stop the police van from leaving the scene.

The Reynolds brothers were later arraigned at William Street Magistrate's Court, where they were subsequently released on $100 bail after being bound over to keep the peace. Speaking to reporters after his arraignment, Millard Reynolds accused Union Minerals of corporate heartlessness:

'We lost a father in their mines. We lost our homes. We lost a community. And what has Union Minerals done to compensate us? Nothing. They let the state put us in sub-standard accommodation. They stopped our wages. They haven't offered a penny of compensation to any of the bereaved families. As far as I'm concerned, they're nothing but a bunch of pygmies.'

'Daddy and Les never went to jail,' Krystal said, 'because Union Minerals started getting all sorts of bad publicity about their treatment of the miners, so they asked the courts to drop all charges. And eventually they did pay some sort of compensation – five thousand dollars to every Wollanup family, plus an additional ten thousand to the widows of the three men who were killed. A pittance, really. Especially since we really had lost our entire secure little world.

'Worst yet, all the mining jobs in Kalgoorlie were filled at the time. Which meant that people started heading off to any part of the country where there was employment – and the whole Wollanup community simply broke up. Daddy moved us all to Perth where he found work in a garage, and Mum did some cleaning in a local hotel. Then Les followed with his family and then Uncle Robbo, and one day the two of them talked their way on to the night-shift at this abattoir near Fremantle. Finally, Gus showed up, somehow managed to get himself accepted for the pre-med course at the local Uni – but ended up dropping out and started hanging up with some druggies, dealing grass. Made pretty good money at it too. Even though – like Daddy and the rest of them – he hated the city and kept talking about somehow getting back to Wollanup.'

She glanced at her watch, then became very businesslike, gathering up the newspaper clippings, taking care of the plates. 'Better stop now – before Angie comes tripping in. I'll show you the rest on Saturday. You like steak?'

' 'Roo steak?'

'Filet steak. Les said that he's put two aside for me in his freezer. We could have them as our alternative to the garbage barbie. What d'you say?'

'Roll on Saturday.'

Angie was pleased that Krystal had forced me into the shower. 'Fuck me, he's all clean and shiny' was her one drunken comment on the subject. But I still remained zonked whenever she was around, longing for six p.m. Saturday to arrive.

Krystal showed up bang on time – and Angie instantly rushed out the door, saying, 'I'm gonna be real late, okay?' When she was safely up the road, Krystal put her bag on the kitchen table and pulled out a wad of wax paper. Unwrapping it, she revealed two perfectly cut circles of red meat, each around two inches thick.

'Beautiful, aren't they?' she said – and I noticed that her hair was freshly washed and that she was wearing an exotic scent. Patchouli, perhaps. She began to unpack the rest of the bag, showing off an amazing array of fresh produce.

'The menu for dinner this evening is: pan-fried filet steak, fresh celery braised in garlic butter, fresh tomato salad. And a bottle of Cape Mentelle Cabernet Sauvignon – a great drop. But first . . . how 'bout making another trip to the shower? You're ponging again, mate.'

Five minutes under the cold spray was about all I could take – but I did feel better for it. And instead of throwing on another grubby T-shirt and shorts, I reached into the foot-locker and changed into my best clothes: an old Brooks Brothers white Oxford shirt and a pair of Gap khakis. It was the first time I'd worn long trousers since setting foot in Oz.

'A new man,' Krystal said, looking me over. 'You human again?'

'Getting there.'

'This should help you along,' she said, handing me a glass of the blood-red wine.

I put the glass to my nose and breathed deeply. My head tingled at the complexity of the bouquet. And then I took the most meagre of sips.

During the Beirut hostage crisis, I remember reading

somewhere that one of the released French captives had just published a little book on wine. It wasn't a taster's handbook or one of those 'Bordeaux for Three Bucks a Bottle' guides. Instead it was a study of wine as spiritual sustenance: the metaphysics of a good Chablis, that kind of very French thing. But when that first tiny mouthful of Cape Mentelle Cab Sauv electrified my palate, I suddenly understood why the abstract idea of wine could have such resonance for a man held against his will. It wasn't the alcoholic kick of the wine that made it so emotionally potent; rather, the way its subtle intricacy reminded you of the more exalted things in life – and, in the process, pointed up the need to somehow transcend the hardship of your own situation. Spirituality, after all, is all about the search for some rarefied state beyond your mundane existence. And a glass or two of kick-ass Cab Sauv, I decided, was not a bad way of getting there.

The dinner was also an exercise in sublime escapism. Krystal had laid a proper table, with two china plates, linen napkins and placemats. She'd brought the only classical record in Wollanup (the Mozart Clarinet Concerto), put it on the record player and lit a candle. When she turned off the fluorescent lights, this dump called home was bathed in a soft, flickering glow. Then she brought over the steaks – superbly seared on the outside, cool and pink within. The vegetables were just as elegant – the celery delicately braised, the tomatoes dressed in a light vinaigrette with just a hint of basil. We ate slowly and in reverential silence, not wanting to disturb the aura of enchantment, the illusion that we had somehow eluded our grim circumstances. This was not a meal; this was High Church.

'I'm afraid I couldn't find any real coffee,' she said, 'but I brought the Marlboros back.'

'You are amazing,' I said.

'Hardly,' she said. As she dug into her bag, I could see she was blushing. 'I also brought these back as well,' she said, handing me two newspaper clippings.

The first was a biggie – the front page of the weekend section of *The Melbourne Age*, dated 16 May 1983. Across the top of the page was a large photograph of Daddy (looking marginally younger, but still ape-like and threatening), standing alone in the empty, windswept main street of Wollanup. Below this was the headline:

DEATH OF A TOWN
by Kirstin Keeler

He came back for the funeral - the burial of the town which three generations of his family called home. For last Saturday, the federal government in Canberra decreed that the Great Victoria Desert mining hamlet of Wollanup was null and void as a community. And for Millard Reynolds – born and raised in Wollanup like his parents and grandparents before him – it was like mourning the death of a loved one.

It was the Federal Minister for Mines and Mineral Resources, Mr Ron Browning (Lab., Port Hedland) who sounded the death knell for Wollanup, when he issued a statement last Friday that the town – which had not been inhabited since a mine explosion in 1979 – would no longer be regarded as part of either state or federal infrastructure . . .

'Of course, that wasn't the last time Daddy visited Wollanup – he would pop out there every so often with Les or Robbo or Gus, making certain that no itinerants or aborigines had moved in and taken it over. At the time, all four of our families were living together in these two adjoining houses in Fremantle, and the atmosphere was like one big commune. Lots of naked kids running around, lots of grass being smoked, lots of alternative plans being hatched. And I recall Daddy and the three boys getting together several times over some big fat joint and dreaming big dreams about moving back to Wollanup. Creating their own separate society, cut off from the rest of the country. A real collective society, free from money grubbing, avarice and all that other greedy stuff which has made Australia what it is today. They had the town just waiting there to be reoccupied – what they needed was a small industry or business that could fund it, yet not draw too much attention to the fact that people were back living in a place which the federal government had declared no longer habitable.'

Krystal said that, around this time, a grandmother or two died off and the family came into a little money – maybe $20,000 – which they put aside for the big exodus back to Wollanup. And then, in 1986, Robbo came home from work one morning, all excited, saying how he'd met this bloke named Jones at the abattoir, who was just opening up a pet food factory in Kalgoorlie and was looking for someone in that part of the state to supply him with butchered 'roo meat.

Within days, Jones was over at their house, talking money. After driving him out to Wollanup one weekend – and showing him an old warehouse that would be perfect as a little abattoir – the boys actually struck a bargain with him: in exchange for an initial investment in some meat-processing equipment, they'd be his exclusive supplier of dead 'roos and charge him rock-bottom prices for the meat – 50 per cent less than any other slaughterhouse. And they also wouldn't have to hit him with a Government Sales Tax because they would be a phantom company – operating from a town which, as far as anybody in authority knew, was no longer functioning.

I turned to the final clipping. It was from Australia's main weekly news magazine, *The Bulletin*. Second of August 1986 – to the best of Krystal's knowledge, the last time the name 'Wollanup' ever appeared in print. It was a short piece, from what appeared to be their Diary column.

NOW YOU SEE IT, NOW YOU DON'T

Last week, a town literally fell off the map, when the
Royal Australian Automobile Club published their new
road atlas. One astute observer in our office noticed that
the Great Victoria Desert mining town of Wollanup –
closed down by the federal government after a 1979
asbestos mine explosion – no longer merited mention on
the RAAC's new regional map of Western Australia.
Gone, too, was any sign of the unsealed 320k track that
connected Wollanup to the single-lane Kalgoorlie
Highway. According to the RAAC's chief cartographer,
Reginald Caton-Jones, the decision to excise Wollanup
from the map was taken because, 'It's a ghost town in
the actual back-of-beyond. Which means that, quite
frankly, it simply doesn't exist any more. And if a town
no longer exists, then it has no business on our map.'

'We moved almost immediately after that story appeared,'
Krystal said, 'because now we knew that nobody would ever
come snooping around Wollanup again. So we closed down
our lives in Fremantle, told neighbours and teachers that our
fathers had found jobs out East, packed one bag each, and left
one night. Never to return.'

'Didn't any of you object?' I asked.

'We were all made to believe that it was going to be a great
adventure. Summer camp all year round.'

'You bought into this fantasy too?'

'Absolutely. I was in my first year of teacher training college, I had a surfer boyfriend named Dave and spent a lot of
time at the beach. But when Daddy came to me and said,
"We're gonna need you as the schoolteacher in Wollanup", I
couldn't say no. Family is family, after all. And anyway, the
idea of starting up an entire town again struck me as rather
romantic. Especially as it was my hometown too.

'And for the first few years, we all did feel a bit like pio-
neers. Having to make do with basic amenities, basic food.

Learning to live without things like television and movies. Getting used to being back in the middle of nowhere. None of us minded, really – because we still all thought it was such a great thing, having a town all to ourselves, where we could make our own rules and say to hell with the rest of the world.'

But though Daddy and his cronies had worked out clever things like the chit system – and also made a success of the meat-processing business – they hadn't considered one very obvious social problem when they were planning their communal dream: what were all their kids eventually going to do for spouses as they started getting older? It was your Angie who started all the trouble. When she was nineteen, Les found her one night in the chicken coop, having a quickie with one of Robbo's teenage sons.'

I choked on a lungful of smoke. And said, 'She was screwing one of her cousins?'

'You know Pete – the bloke whose job it is to decapitate the 'roos? He was the one.'

'But she told me . . .'

'What?'

'. . . that I was . . .'

'*The first*?' Her voice was loud with incredulity. 'And you *believed* her?'

'Guess I did,' I said weakly.

'Bloody men,' she said. 'All full of bluster and cockiness. Until it comes to sex – at which point you all get hopelessly witless. You weren't the first, mate. You weren't even the second, third, fourth or fifth. Angie was kind of the town mattress – the Wollanup sex education course for most of her male cousins, until Les found her and Pete in the barn. At which point, there was hell to pay – especially when it turned out she was pregnant.'

I had another coughing fit.

'What happened to the baby?' I asked.

'She had a miscarriage after two months – which, as you can imagine, was a relief for everyone. But all our parents were still rather concerned. Because they realized that it was only a matter of time before someone else got pregnant by one of their cousins . . . or worse yet, a brother. And if they didn't do something to stop this inter-family sex, then the next generation of children in Wollanup would probably be a bunch of mutants.

'So that's when they called a big town meeting and informed us that anyone caught doing it with a relative would be severely punished – like the beating you saw Charlie get during your first week here. But they also promised us that, when we each turned twenty-one, we would be allowed to leave Wollanup for six to eight weeks, travel around and find a spouse to bring back home.'

I said, 'They couldn't really have expected all their kids to remain virgins until they were twenty-one?'

'Of course they knew that – hormones being hormones – their kids were gonna play around. But they hoped that, by having this no-sex rule on the books, they might be just able to keep potential in-breeding under control. And they figured that, once everybody started growing up and bringing newcomers into the community, then the problem would finally go away.'

'So I was the second newcomer kidnapped into the community?'

'No, you were Number Four. Ever talk to Janine and Carey? They're married to Robbo's sons, Ron and Greg. Janine was a checkout girl at a supermarket in Perth; Carey used to work at a McDonald's in Brisbane. The two boys met them on their separate travels, proposed marriage and life in a tiny nowhere town, they accepted and came here quite happily?'

'You mean they weren't drugged?'

'No need. They wanted to be married, they met a guy they liked, end of story. Of course, when it comes to Janine and Carey, we're not exactly dealing with major brain-power – which is probably another reason why they've settled in so well. But still, everyone was very pleased with how those two matches had worked out – and thought that this system of bringing outsiders into Wollanup was going to succeed just fine.' She paused to drain the dregs of her wine. 'Then it was my turn to find a man.'

She blew out the candle and turned on the overhead light. The romance of the dinner was washed out in a crackle of fluorescent tubes. We were back in my home, the hole.

'Time for a little walk,' Krystal said, dumping the packet of Marlboros and my stubbed-out butts into her bag. 'Think you can manage one?'

'I can try.'

Outside, a full moon softened the dark vacancy of a Wollanup night and gave us enough light to see by.

'They haven't torched the mountain yet,' she said, looking towards town, from which floated the scent of spit-roasted animal flesh and the garrulous buzz of heavy public boozing. 'You don't mind missing it, do you?'

'You must be joking.'

She steered me away from the village, walking the few yards beyond my house to where the road ended. Then she led me into the open tableland beyond the town, keeping me steady as we crunched through gravelly dirt. I shambled along – my legs still rickety after eight days of inertia – until Krystal brought me to a tiny patch of land that had been raked smooth of rock. In the middle of this plot was a narrow mound of earth, around six foot long. A grave.

Krystal looked at it long and hard. Then said, 'Jack. I met him on the beach in Perth. He was a tall, scraggly bloke, with sandy hair and bad teeth and a brilliant laugh. Just finished his English degree at Uni in Sydney and was knocking around the country for a year or so, trying to figure out what to do next. Fancied himself a writer, but admitted he was too lazy to get anything down on paper. A real "no worries" type. Good fun.

'Anyway, we started hanging out together. Spent nearly

three weeks living on the beach and got along so great I started thinking, "This could work". So I told him all about Wollanup and he sounded really keen on the communal idea of the place and said, sure, he'd drive me home, as he had no plans and always wanted to travel into the real bush.

'The trip back was a nightmare. Three days in his clapped-out Holden, which kept overheating. And as soon as he saw the town, his reaction was the same as yours: "What a dump". So after about forty-eight hours, he packed his bag and told me that, much as he liked me, he really couldn't handle the garbage mountain or anything else about this place. I didn't stop him – much as I didn't want to see him go – but as soon as he tried to drive up the hill, Daddy and the boys were out in force. With guns. Blocking his way.

' "What the hell is going on?" he said. Daddy told him, "You're not leaving – you're staying here and marrying my daughter". Jack called him crazy, Daddy slapped him across the face and said, "She didn't bring you here for a visit, mate. She was sent out to find a husband, and you're it."

'I was only standing a few feet away. And after Daddy said that, Jack turned to me with this look on his face – I'll never forget it – that was pure hate. Then he brushed Daddy aside, jumped into his car and tried to roar off, even though Robbo and Gus both chased the car. Daddy fired a warning shot over the roof. But when Jack kept going, he took aim at the rear windscreen and let go with two shots. The glass blew out, the car suddenly stopped, the horn started blaring. And when we all rushed up, there was Jack slumped against the wheel. The back of his head was missing.'

From the distance came a loud inebriated countdown – *five, four, three, two, one* – then an eruptive rumble as the garbage mountain went up in flame. It sent crazed orange salvos of fire across the sky, like a volley of deranged fireworks. Soon, all of Wollanup seemed awash in its radiance. It was an inferno for a true hell.

'So that's why Les gives me all that good meat and wine on

the quiet,' Krystal said. 'Because, like everybody else here, he feels guilty about what happened to Jack. Everybody except Daddy. "Jack had to die", he told me, "because if he'd gotten out, he would've told the police about us and that would have been the end of Wollanup".'

'Jack's death still didn't stop him from sending Angie up north in search of a husband. But instead of nabbing some dense bushman who'd fit in here – like everybody advised her to do – she showed up with you. And the morning I saw you emerge out of the chicken coop . . . I knew that I'd have to get you out of here.'

She locked her arm with mine. 'And that's what I'm going to do.'

I looked at her carefully. 'You have a plan?'

'Yeah,' she said. 'I have a plan.'

'So . . . tell me.'

'Later, mate. Later.'

We turned back to the conflagration.

'Hell of a fire,' I said.

'Hell of a fire.'

'Krystal . . .'

'Mmn . . .'

'What's rule number one of Outback life?'

'Never drive after dark – you might hit a 'roo.'

'Good advice,' I said.

part three

one

She said, 'Explain to me how a rotor arm works.'

I said, 'It's a little piece of Bakelite with four wires, housed inside a distributor cap. When a car ignition is turned on, the rotor arm whizzes around, distributing electricity to the spark plugs, which causes the engine to fire. Without the rotor arm, the car is immobile. Impossible to start.'

She said, 'Do you know how to rebuild a rotor arm?'

I said, 'Never tried.'

She said, 'You'll have to try now.'

There were only three working vehicles in the village – the Wollanup Meats refrigeration truck, a transit van which Les took on his supply runs, and the open-back lorry used for the daily 'roo cull. They were, she said, all kept under heavy lock and key in a pair of sheds at the back of the meat-processing plant. Whenever they were not in use, the rotor arms in the distributor caps were removed. Les kept the arms locked up in his safe – ensuring that there was no way anyone could make a run for it in one of those vehicles.

But even if someone did manage to get a van started in the middle of the night, they wouldn't get very far. Because there was a secret rotating night watch – made up of Les's and Robbo's sons. They took turns staying up all night, sitting in a lookout post on the roof of the pub, making certain no one was on the road after closing time. They liked the work – because it earned them an extra six beer chits per watch.

'They were all put on high alert when you were rebuilding your microbus,' Krystal said, 'just in case you tried to do a run-ner. And they were a bit disappointed that you didn't make a break for it.'

'Knew I didn't have a chance,' I said. 'Because there was no way that I could drive up that hill without being noticed.'

'You're one smart guy,' she said.

Like me, she'd been timing how long it took a van to strug-gle up that jarring road. Les's van was the fastest – around forty-seven minutes to reach the plateau above us – but it had four-wheel drive. The fridge truck and the 'roo lorry, being significantly larger, laboured for well over an hour, never accelerating more than 15mph on a track that was a axle-bend-ing collection of pot-holes and cavities. And being a twenty-year-old heap of shit, the 'roo lorry inevitably broke down a couple of times a year – forcing Tom and Rock to trek down the hill and leave the day's kill festering in the back.

'Now when the 'roo lorry conks out,' Krystal said, 'the boys always remove the rotor arm before hiking back to town. I know this, because I've seen them turn it over to Les in the shop. And Daddy will never head up the hill to repair the lorry until dawn the next morning, because it's just too hot to carry out repairs in open bush after 10 a.m. There's no shade up there at all.'

'He won't go up after sunset?' I asked.

'It's too dark to work – even with a couple of powerful torches.'

'Think I see what you're getting at,' I said.

'You're one very smart guy,' she said.

Her plan was sharp. Real sharp. It involved me putting together a spare rotor arm, hiding it, then waiting until the 'roo lorry broke down again up on the ridge. As soon as that happened, we'd be on our way that night – sneaking out of our respective homes an hour or so after the pub closed at eleven, using back alleys to avoid being spotted by the night watch atop the pub, making our way up the hill by foot.

'Three hours should get us to the top,' Krystal said.

'Budget for four.'

'Are you that out of shape?'

'Absolutely.'

'Okay, mud-guts – I'll give you the extra hour. Which means we should probably reach the van by 4.15, 4.30 at the latest. How long do you think it would take to get it started?'

'Depends what caused it to break down.'

'Gather the problem's usually minor things like a broken fan-belt or a short in the alternator.'

'Then you better allow another hour before we get moving – especially as I'll have to fit the new rotor arm too.'

'That would make it 5.30. Daddy would already be halfway up the hill in Les's van. Which means that even if we did get away, he'd only be around fifteen minutes behind us. We need a lot more lead time than that.'

I took a reflective drag or two off my Marlboro.

'Say Daddy was sick that morning. So sick that he somehow couldn't get up?'

'Tell me more,' she said.

We couldn't talk for much longer, as the garbage barbie was finally breaking up and all the drunks were staggering home. Once again, Krystal dumped the Marlboros and the contents of the ashtray into her bag while briskly briefing me on my next moves:

'Keep acting unwell for a few more days. Then eventually get back to work at the garage, but maintain the sad-sack look, so everyone will think you've finally accepted your fate here. Start reconstructing your microbus again, but in the meantime try to get sifting through that mountain of junk out by Daddy's shed. He broke up Jack's Holden after he died, and I'm sure the distributor cap must be there somewhere. If it is, then we're on our way.'

'Only if the rotor arm is repairable,' I said, 'and if it can also fit the distributor cap of the 'roo lorry.'

'It should,' she said. 'The lorry's a Holden too.'

'It's still a real long shot.'

'Yeah – but it's our only shot.'

Angie crashed through the door a few minutes later. Krystal was at the sink, drying her hands after putting the last of our dishes away. I was back on the bed, curled up in my favourite ante-natal position.

'So,' Angie said, 'you guys hump a lot tonight?'

She belched. A long precarious belch. Then she collapsed in a stupor on the bed. Krystal yelled in her ear a few times, but to no avail. Angie was gonzo. I was about to speak, but Krystal put a finger to her lips to remind me that I must play the mute for few more days. Then, with a quick wave, she slipped out into the night.

I looked at the lump beside me, now snoring like a hibernating grizzly. I will find that rotor arm, I *must* find that rotor arm.

I went back to work four days later – having finally grown tired of lying on my bed for most of the day, staring into space, listening to Angie sing 'I Like to Be in America' as *West Side Story* blared on the record player for the eighty-eighth time. On this first morning back, I simply nodded to Daddy, walked into the shed and got down to the business of sifting through the debris of my microbus. After around twenty minutes, the gorilla lumbered over, stood in the doorway and watched as I scoured the floor for missing engine parts.

'So Yank-wank, no longer acting the hatter?'

I kept rummaging, my eyes at ground-level.

He didn't like my lack of response and grew testy. 'Expect to see that van as good as new again, y'understand?'

I looked up, making certain my stare was a vacant one.

'Yes,' I said, in what I hoped sounded like a haunted whisper, and then returned to my manic search for lost parts.

'Fuckin' spas,' he said under his breath and left.

I maintained this in-another-cosmos behaviour both at home and at work. I answered my wife and employer in monosyllables ('Yes', 'No', and 'Okay' being the extent of my repartee). I never stared them directly in the face, but always made sure I was looking way beyond them – as if I was trying to get a fix on the planet Pluto. However, I did start eating solid food again, I did start smoking again, and (much to Angie's chagrin, since she really had been drinking for two) I did start using my beer chits again. But while in the pub, I engaged in no small talk. I just sat on my stool, looked into my beer, and let a smouldering roll-up droop from my lips. Other drinkers would try to engage me in conversation, but I'd just smile shyly and stare back down into the bottom of my glass.

The result of all this concentrated play acting was – as I'd hoped – a communal sense of guilt about the state of my mental health. I wanted the good folk of Wollanup to believe I was a broken man – so psychologically incapacitated that I posed no threat as a potential escapee. And I wanted them to take Daddy to task for his treatment of me.

I knew I was succeeding in this campaign when Gladys (of all people) lashed out at her husband one night on my behalf. I was sitting in the pub, perched on my usual stool, when my parents-in-law rolled in for a drink. I didn't acknowledge their arrival, I just preserved my now-standard look of permanent vacancy.

'Feel like a beer, Yank?' Gladys called over, her voice full of maternal concern.

I gave her my best loopy smile and shouted back, 'Gosh!

Thanks! No!' Then I shuffled off to the toilet, muttering to myself.

As soon as I was out of the bar, she was verbally boxing his ears.

'Proud of yourself, big man?' she said. 'Happy with your handiwork?'

'Not my fault he's round the twist.'

'Not half. Everybody blames you for what's happened to the Yank. Everybody. Even your precious little Princess. Y'should have heard her when she came to the house today. Almost in tears she was, saying how the Yank was starting to do great here until you jiggered his van. Saying how she heard he did a beaut job and you fucked it up because you're a crap mechanic and can't handle seeing someone do real quality work. Saying that she's starting to go troppo, living with a zombie. A zombie you created.'

Standing at the urinal, I could hear the sheepishness in his voice as he said, 'She's not really angry with me, is she?'

'You fucking berk,' Gladys roared.

And the next morning, when he saw me sniffing around his precious personal cache of spares and junk, he didn't order me away (as he had done in the past), but hesitantly asked, 'You looking for anything?'

'Parts,' I said, barking the word.

'For your van?'

'Yeah. The van. Okay?'

'Guess so,' he said, not trying to hide his reluctance. 'Just don't leave the place in a mess.'

Don't leave it in a mess? Daddy's personal junk pile was an incurable mess – a ton or two of debris scattered over half an acre. Trying to find the Holden's distributor cap in this tangle of rubble was going to be an impossible task – especially as I figured that he would only tolerate me burrowing through his prized trash for three days at the most. I decided that my best shot was trying to locate the Holden's engine block, and hope that the distributor cap was still attached to it. But whether I'd even unearth the engine block was questionable, as I was overwhelmed by the sheer volume of junk it was buried under. For around an hour I circled the pile, trying to see if I could somehow spot it amidst the debris. No joy. Then I reluctantly got down to some real dirty work and started sifting through the heap piece by piece.

After five hours, I had discovered three car-doors, a twisted steering column, a smashed cistern, some masonry bricks, dozens of rusted rivets, eight lengths of copper tubing, a glove-compartment door, a disembowelled car-seat, one head-lamp, an old toaster, three used alternators, an assortment of torn fan-belts and no engine block. All of my arm and back muscles felt besieged, while the sun had done a splendid job of stewing my brain. I held a water hose over my head for a few minutes, then retired to the pub.

Two beers helped dampen my rage and disappointment at having found nothing. As I motioned for a third tinny, Gus sidled in and climbed on to the stool beside me.

'How's the ace mechanic?' he asked, all friendly.

'Yeah, well, hey.' I was becoming a very practised simpleton.

'Think you and I need to have a talk,' Gus said. 'A little medical rap. Could you come by the house now?'

'Beer first,' and drained my glass in one long swig, allowing some of it to cascade down my chin.

'Yum, yum,' I woofed. Gus looked uncomfortable.

'Shall we split?' he asked.

'Doctor time?' I shouted.

'That's right,' he said. 'Doctor time.'

Gus's house was only marginally larger than my own. There was an extra kid's room with seven mattresses on the floor, a couple of hammocks stretched across the main living area, old discoloured posters of Janis and Jimi and The Grateful Dead, a long rough-hewn table (scene of his famous triumph as a surgeon), and a tiny alcove which functioned as the Wollanup medical centre. Gus motioned me to sit in one of the two beanbags in his consulting room. Then he opened the door of a little fridge and – after digging behind assorted vaccine vials and pill bottles – he managed to unearth two cans of beer.

'Have another coldie,' he said.

'Yum, yum.'

'Y'know, everyone's kind of worried about you, Nick-o,' he said.

'Nice.'

'It's not nice – 'cause no one wants to see you flipped out. You sleeping at all?'

'Sleep?'

'You're not sleeping?'

'Need no sleep.'

'You need a lot of sleep. Cool you right out. Lack of sleep's probably half your problem. You feeling depressed too?'

I shrugged, then looked like I was on the verge of tears.

'Right – I think we're getting somewhere. Now I'm gonna give you some real good drugs that are gonna help you crash at night and keep you cheery by day. The happy pills are called Valium and they produce one beautiful high; and then you're gonna pop two Halcion with a beer before beddy-bye and slip off into real sweet dreams. Follow the prescription, and I guarantee you won't just be back to normal in a week, you'll be *too normal*.'

I thanked Gus in my own hesitant way, pocketed the pills, then stored them at home in a hiding place I'd created behind the lavatory.

On my way into work the next morning, I saw Krystal in the road. She said, 'Morning', I waved back, and as we passed each other I quickly whispered, 'Got the drugs.'

She acknowledged this news with a fast smile, but kept walking on. We'd hardly spoken to each other since the night of the garbage barbie – on the grounds that, if we were seen regularly in each other's company, Daddy and Co. might get suspicious. So we maintained our distance – but passed on information every morning with a murmur or a nod.

And when I passed her at sunrise during the next two days, my 'Hello' was followed by a quick shake of the head. Because my hunt for the distributor cap had still turned up nothing.

The next morning, while I was digging my way through four busted mattresses and a stack of old baking tins, I looked up and saw Tom and Rock walking down the hill. Above them, on the empty plateau, stood the lorry. Motionless. Immobile. Broken-down.

I grew frantic. Tearing apart the bottomless junk heap, I had one last desperate search for the engine block before the two boys walked into the garage. From where they were on the hill, I figured I had an hour's grace – but it was to no avail. Though I had now uncovered the Holden's windscreen, its back-seat and one wheel, the key to my escape still eluded me. And my heart sank when I heard approaching footsteps, followed by Rock's voice yelling, 'Hey, Daddy, the lorry's fucked again.'

When I saw Krystal on the road the next morning, I whispered one word: 'Sorry.'

She shrugged and glanced up at the ridge, where the lorry was now moving again. Half an hour later, as I was excavating three bushels of wire fencing, Daddy drove up in Les's van.

'Those stupid shits,' he said, getting out of the cab. 'Know what the problem was? Flooded engine and a couple of dirty points. Made me go up there for nothing.'

'Good now?'

'Could use a service. They're bringing it in as soon as they've dropped the 'roos off.'

'Need a hand with it?'

'That rust-bucket's my baby. You just finish up looking for your parts. Haven't you found what you need by now?'

'Almost.'

'Well, I want you to clear out of my junk pile by tomorrow, get back to your shed and get on with rebuilding your van. Got me?'

I dragged myself back to the heap and hauled away another

bushel or two of wire. Still no goddamn engine block. Then I took a step forward to tackle some copper piping. As I did, I heard a distinctive crack and glanced down to see what appeared to be a black plastic mug beneath my foot.

The distributor cap. Now fractured in half.

I wanted to cry, scream, commit first-degree murder. But when I picked it up and removed the plastic shell, the rotor arm was still intact. A little bent, but easily fixable. Looking around to make certain Daddy wasn't watching, I popped the rotor in the pocket of my shorts, buried the broken distributor cap back in the rubble and walked over to where my boss was half-hidden beneath the hood of the 'roo lorry. I took a long look at the engine block and felt something close to euphoria – the lorry's distributor cap was the same as the one I had just stepped on.

'Bad shape?' I asked.

'Needs new plugs, points, oil filter, new clutch cable, new fan-belt. But when I get done with her, she shouldn't have a problem for months. Maybe even a year.'

'Great,' I said weakly.

I went to the pub, drank myself stupid, staggered home, and remembered to hide the rotor arm behind the toilet before passing out.

I slept late the next morning, but made certain I ran into Krystal as she left the schoolhouse after classes.

'Found it,' I whispered as she passed by.

She slammed on the brakes. 'You're joking.'

'No.'

'And . . .'

'It should work,' I said.

A careful smile from Krystal.

'Now what?' I said.

'We just wait.'

two

Daddy may have been a crap mechanic, but the 'roo lorry didn't break down for another four months.

Every morning, as I left my house and walked the ten minutes to the garage, my eyes would fix on the road leading up the hill. Every morning, I expected to see Tom and Rock stumbling down that path, cursing the bloody lorry while I silently celebrated the start of my last day ever in Wollanup. But every morning the lorry went up and down the hill without a hitch. And I had to wait another day. And another day. And another day.

Four months. A third of a year. Such a sizeable block of time. What did I do with it? I drank beer. I watched my wife's belly swell with child. I read every volume in Wollanup's thirty-five book library (including a manual entitled *Modern Abattoir Methods* – that's how desperate I was). I gradually upgraded the state of my mental health – to the point where I decided it was time to hold reasonable conversations again. I watched as Gus went around town, bragging how he'd cured my breakdown. I worked on the resurrection of my van in a haphazard way – because I knew that the moment I finished it, it would be torn apart again. I drank more beer. I waited.

Four months. During my years as a hack in the States, I deliberately squandered time, blowing nearly two decades in shit jobs in shit towns. I didn't care that the years seemed to pass with ever-increasing velocity. I enjoyed frittering away time – because it allowed me to sidestep all the obsessions that propel most people through their day: ambition, family, emotional commitment. So many of my contemporaries talked about 'building a life'. I wasn't interested in building anything. I did my job, I kept my overheads low, I drank my beers, I screwed whatever women I could pick up, I let time pass.

But now – locked into an even more pointless routine – I became aware of time's disturbing preciousness, its inestimable value. And I realized why, in part, I had cracked up after Daddy trashed my van: because I had finally put the time into building something, only then to have it demolished in front of me.

Four months. Maybe all work is about filling time, killing time. But I could now do so much with four months.

'The lorry's bound to break down eventually,' Krystal said, around seven weeks into the wait. It was the night of Rock's twenty-first birthday party and – as I was still regarded as a potential hazard to myself – Krystal was called in to babysit while Angie went off to kill a few brain cells. She showed up with another porta-feast in her string bag: chicken breasts, a head of lettuce, new potatoes, a bottle of Chardonnay and a fifth of cheap French brandy. But first we talked shop, reviewing every facet of our plan, bombarding each other with questions. It was the first time we'd been able to speak at length in over two months and – like any two people with a secret and a limited time to share it – there was a clandestine electricity to our talk.

But finally out came a candle, off went the lights, and the Mozart record got another go-around on the record player. We got tight on the food and the good wine, tighter on the bad brandy, and laughed too much at each other's jokes. A packet of English cigarettes ('Les couldn't get me Marlboros') eventually materialized from her pocket. As I lit one, the flicker of the flame spotlighted her big sad eyes, and I knew I was smitten.

'Are you still in love with Jack?' I suddenly asked, the booze fuelling my imprudence.

'I was never in love with Jack.'

'You weren't?'

'I liked him, of course – but it never developed into anything beyond that. Lack of time.'

'Right,' I said, and there was this long silence between us. Broken finally by Krystal who took my hand in hers, held it against her cheek and said, 'Thank you for asking me that question.'

Another long silence. Only this time neither of us tried to fill it. Because there was no need to.

Revellers snapped the hush. Rock's party was breaking up – and there was the usual chorus of dipsos on the road.

'Dishes,' Krystal whispered and we cleared the table in seconds. As I dumped the plates into the sink, she suddenly threw her arms around me and kissed me with reckless ferocity.

Moments later, she was out the door, and we returned to the play-acting world of keeping our distance, of nods in the road, of waiting for the bloody 'roo lorry to conk out so we could get up that hill and finally stop keeping our distance.

Nine more weeks trudged by. I eventually became so listless with waiting – with the profound tedium of my daily routine – that I took to sleeping late every morning until eight, putting in two hours maximum at the garage, then killing the balance of the day at the pub. And because I wasn't struggling out of bed until several hours after daybreak, I was totally thrown when I sauntered into the garage one Wednesday around ten and found Tom and Rock sitting on a bench, covered in road dirt, looking seriously pissed off.

'What are you guys doing here?' I asked.

'Fuckin' fan-belt,' Rock said. 'Went kaput just when we were starting to load up. Must be twenty dead 'roos up there.'

I had to work hard at containing my nervy excitement. This was it, this was it.

'I'll get you going again in the morning,' Daddy said. 'And the 'roos'll still be there.'

'D'you know what it's like, trying to load a dead 'roo after it's been lying in the sun for a day?' Tom said. 'Fucking grot work.'

'My heart bleeds,' Daddy said. 'Get yourself a coldie and stop shitting bricks.'

I ambled off into my shed, shut the door, picked up one of the VW's smashed-in wings and gave it a few perfunctory knocks with a hammer, trying to keep calm. After a couple of minutes, the door opened and Daddy poked his head in.

'What y'up to?' he asked.

'Panel beating.'

'Going to the pub. Y'coming?'

'Think I'll work on,' I said.

'Want you here early tomorrow. No more of this nine o'clock start, understand?'

'I'll set an alarm.'

As soon as I was certain he'd left the garage, I put aside the dented wing and went to work on the VW engine block, carefully removing its fan-belt. Then I practised putting it back on. The operation took fifteen minutes. Not bad. Add another ten minutes to get the rotor arm in place, and we should have the lorry on the move within a half-hour of reaching it.

I carefully removed the fan-belt again – terrified of tearing

it – then gathered together some basic tools and put the lot
into the little day-pack I carried to work every morning. I
wanted to dash over to Krystal and let her know that we'd
finally gotten the green light, but forced myself to sit down,
have a smoke and kill time – just in case Daddy found it odd
that I was knocking off work so soon after deciding to stay on.

I puffed away madly, trying to downshift myself out of
manic high-gear. Three roll-ups later, I was marginally more
composed, and ready to make my way to the schoolhouse.

Walk, don't run. Act natural. Get that look of jumpy apprehension off your goddamn face. They don't know. Nobody
knows but Krystal.

'Morning,' I said as I walked into the schoolroom, just as
her pupils were gathering their books at the end of the day's
lessons.

'G'day,' she said, her smile tight and nervous.

'You got that copy of *Tale of Two Cities* you said you'd lend
me?'

Her eyes widened, but she stuck to the script. 'Damn. Left
it at home. Tomorrow?'

'Sure,' I said. 'Tomorrow.'

End of coded conversation. I made a brisk about-face and
walked as fast as I could back to my house – for I saw that the
meat processing plant was emptying and figured that Angie
would only be a few minutes behind me. After hiding my day-
pack in the cavity behind the loo, I withdrew the two vials of
Valium and Halcion. I ground down the ten pills in each con-
tainer, poured half back into one vial, the rest into a salt shaker
I had stolen from the pub, and entombed the lot again.

Angie arrived home seconds later. We made small talk.

'Good day at the office, dear?' I asked.

'Not enough 'roos, since the lorry broke down. And this
one bloke I was gutting (she always referred to kangaroo
cadavers as "blokes") had the thickest bloody intestine I'd
ever seen.'

End of small talk. We had a nap. And later on – at her

insistence – we had a quickie. She was on top, and with every thrust and lunge, the weight of our child-to-be pummelled my stomach. My lasting bequest to Wollanup: a half-Yank conceived in stupidity. A kid I'd never see – and would think about every day for the rest of my life.

'I'm cooking tonight,' I said later.

'What you gonna make me?'

' 'Roo burgers.'

'Beaut. Make sure mine is really well done. With a lot of salt.'

'You got it.'

Her burger was very heavily seasoned – with a large pinch of the Valium/Halcion powder. I had retrieved a vial during a trip to the bog and sprinkled it generously over the meat while Angie was taking a shower. Just to make certain that she slept very well, I also added a double-pinch of drugs to a glass of beer that I handed her when she emerged from the bathroom.

There was no noxious after-taste to this seasoning, as Angie downed the beer in one go and actually complimented me on the burger. I had managed to delay serving dinner until nine (a late mealtime in Wollanup), and ensured that she never had an empty beer can in front of her. By ten, she had her head on the table and was wheezing a comatose wheeze. Bingo. I dumped her on the bed, tucked her in, made a quick trip back to the loo, and set off for the pub.

'Up a little late, aren't you, Yank?' Daddy said, when I walked through the swing doors.

'Can't sleep,' I said.

'Bad dreams?' Daddy taunted.

'All the time.'

It was a thin crowd tonight – just Daddy, Tom and Rock, and Pete – his pitted face and stringy hair still lightly flecked with animal blood (he really did look like the sort of creepy hayseed who would enjoy banging his cousin in a chicken coop). Pete's presence in the bar at this hour could only mean one thing – he was on night watch. Which meant that I really did owe the guy a beer.

'It's my shout,' I announced to this quartet. 'Who's got a thirst?'

As they all turned to Les and yelled for a beer on my tab, I slipped the druggy salt shaker out of my pocket and put it on the bar, next to another shaker of exactly the same make.

'Good on ya, Yank,' Rock said.

'Yeah, much obliged,' Pete said.

After Les poured out my beer, I grabbed the shaker and started salting it.

'What you doing there?' Pete asked.

'Old American trick. Gives it a decent head. Want to try?'

I shoved the other shaker filled with powdered tranquillizers along the bar. To my total relief, Pete not only took the bait, but the drugs actually did revitalize the head on the beer (though I did have to encourage him to 'salt it' rather heavily). Tom and Rock also gave it a go, but when the shaker finally worked its way down to Daddy, he said, 'Ain't putting no fucking salt in my beer.'

Danger, danger.

'Won't hurt it, right, guys?' I said.

They grunted agreement.

'Just makes the head foamier.'

'Like it flat,' Daddy said, emptying his glass. 'And I don't need no Yank telling me how to drink beer.'

I was back at the house within a half-hour, thinking: blown it, blown it. But there was no time to bemoan this fuck-up. At least Pete had 'tranqued' his beer and should be fast asleep on the pub roof by now.

I glanced at my watch. It was time. I went to the loo and cleared out my makeshift safe. I did a quick inventory of my day-pack – rotor arm, fan-belt, tools, passport – and added the house flashlight and a change of clothes I had left balled up on a chair earlier. And I also grabbed a book which I'd bought in Darwin and had sat on a shelf in my van until Angie moved it in here. Fortunately, Angie hated crime writing, for had she cracked open this Penguin edition of Raymond Chandler's *Trouble is My Business*, she would have found hidden within its pages my Visa card, my refund docket for AMEX traveller's cheques, my plane ticket home.

Hoisting the pack, I walked over to the bed, clapped my hands twice, barked Angie's name in her ear. Nothing. With the dose I'd given her, she'd be out until well into the morning. And then . . .

I wondered how she'd react to my departure. Fury? Hatred – especially when she was told that Krystal had run off with me? A little grief, perhaps? Not at losing me per se, but at losing the doofus in the house, the lump on the bed – the companion who, for better or worse, was there at night, whom you told about your day, who gave you the illusion that you really weren't all alone in the world.

Part of me wanted to kiss her goodbye. Part of me wanted to beat her skull in with a chair. In the end, I just shook my head at the random insanity of it all. You make an unneccessary stop at a gas station, you meet someone, your life goes haywire. Fate isn't cruel. Fate is dumb.

I stepped back for one last look, fixing this dump forever in my mind. Then I opened the door.

I was now officially on the run.

three

For the first time in months, the night was overcast. No moon. No stars. No natural light to show me the way out of town. And because the moving beam of a flashlight might attract attention, I had to stumble through the dark.

As I left the house, I crossed over the main road and ducked behind the half-finished shell of a shack under construction. After standing absolutely still for a few moments, making certain that I heard no other footsteps nearby, I moved carefully into the empty plains that encircled Wollanup. I hiked on for around a quarter of a mile until the two or three lights still burning in town appeared distant enough that I considered myself out of earshot. Then I picked up the pace and headed west, trying to concentrate on my footing as I crunched through this gritty prairie. Visions of twisting an ankle – and being discovered here after sunrise, with a rotor arm in my day-pack – made me think hard about every step. Especially as the darkness was so total, so enveloping, that I almost felt as if I was trekking through a terrain without limits, a nebulous infinity.

After a half-hour, the townscape of Wollanup was finally behind me, so I made a right turn. From here it should only have been a five minute walk to the start of the road up the hill. But I blundered around for another half-hour, astray in the murk, my adrenalin in overdrive. I glanced at the luminous hands of my watch. Two-fifteen – some forty-five minutes behind schedule. Shit, shit, shit. But just as I was about to chance detection by using my flashlight, a hand shot out from nowhere and caught me by the face, while another arm grabbed my waist and pulled me to the ground. Heart-attack shock – and when I tried to scream, the hand pressed even harder against my mouth.

'You're late,' Krystal whispered in my ear, now covering my lips with hers.

The kiss was long and crazed – nine weeks of untouchability suddenly being vented in the night air. But before it could edge into anything else, she cut it off.

'We've got to get going,' she said, her voice an edgy murmur. 'Where were you?'

'Lost.'

'I thought you'd blown it.'

'I may have. Daddy wouldn't salt his beer.'

'Oh, God . . .' she said, grabbing my wrist to glance at my watch. 'He'll be up in two and a half hours.'

'Still want to chance it?'

'I'm not waiting another four months,' she said. 'Can you make it?'

'Got no choice,' I said – and we set off.

It is amazing what you can achieve when you are under the threat of grievous bodily harm. Though you may be an aerobic disaster with nicotine-cured lungs, you somehow find the stamina needed for double-timing it up an 1,100-foot hill in pitch darkness. But it was still a hellish climb. The road was one long brutal obstacle course – with a 40 gradient and potholes. Twice, I tumbled, the second time, my right shin scraping the corner of a jagged rock. No blood – but I nearly bit my lip in half, suppressing a yelp. Even healthy, cigarette-free Krystal found the trek hard-going – and we had to make repeated stops all the way up, quickly depleting the meagre water supplies in her canteen.

Time also began to evaporate. By four, we were just at the halfway point. By five – Daddy's wake-up hour – the lorry still seemed a long way off. And when we finally staggered on to the plateau twenty minutes later, dawn light was seeping through the opaque sky.

There was a smell of death up there – that acrid fragrance of decomposing animal flesh. The lorry was now fifty feet in front of us, but to get there we had to wade through a pile of kangaroo corpses which covered the landscape. They weren't just the left-behinds from the previous day's kill; there must have been two hundred or more carcasses which Tom and Rock had previously failed to transport down the hill, abandoning them to rot where slain. Many of them were virtual skeletons; others were tangles of rotted meat, already half-eaten by the swarm of buzzards who, with first light, had now gathered above us. They were in a holding pattern – unwilling to swoop down as long as we were amongst their prey – but still doing their best to spook us away. They serenaded us with threatening squawks. They circled around in ever-tightening hoops. They let loose with a barrage of chalky droppings, scoring direct hits on our heads and shoulders.

We were desperate to get out of this nightmare. But it was an appalling slog to the lorry, as every step meant treading on some portion of a decayed corpse (I now understood why Tom and Rock always went to work in knee-high rubber boots). In the end, we simply could take no more of tiptoeing through the carnage and made a run for it, slipping and scrunching our way across the tract of dead animals. Finally reaching the lorry, we jumped into the cab. Krystal was immediately hit with a bad case of the shakes; I had to fight off a strong need to heave. Not that the cab gave us much shelter from the stench – its side windows and rear windscreen were missing and a few of yesterday's cull were piled in the back.

'Christ, no,' Krystal said when she saw our dead companions for the journey ahead.

Then we heard the shots – the distinctive report of a rifle being fired twice into the sky. Scrambling out of the cab we looked down into Wollanup below, and saw that a crowd had gathered, staring up at us. A bulky figure fired into the air again, climbed into a van with another man (also carrying a rifle) and started driving off towards the start of the road. Daddy was en route – and the rifle blasts were simply his way of letting us know that we were in deep, deep trouble.

There was a moment of shared, blind panic – then we got down to business. I popped the hood and began to tackle the fan-belt, while Krystal tried to lighten our load by pulling the half-dozen dead 'roos off the back of the lorry. It was a gruesome task. I looked up briefly from the hood to watch her hauling away a particularly large beast by its ears. Suddenly, she screamed a scream of pure, undistilled shock. When I came running over, I saw that she was covered in blood. The ears had come away in her hands.

We used what little water was left in the canteen to dampen her arms, then mopped up the blood with a grubby rag I found in the glove compartment. I expected her to go hide in the cab until I finished my repairs. Instead, she did something that would have been beyond me – she went right back to work, dragging away the remaining 'roos by their feet. Within five minutes, the back of the lorry was cleared.

I was having less success with the fan-belt. The spare I had nicked from the Volkswagen engine was fractionally wider than the Holden's belt, so it didn't slot into the grooves of the two wheels that held it. I kept trying to cram it between these corrugations, but every time I secured half of the belt to the top wheel, it would instantly pop up again when I started stretching it to the bottom one. After five failed attempts, it was my turn to scream – at which point Krystal came over and took charge of the bottom half of the belt. There were two more botched efforts before we managed to edge it into the two sets of grooves – though I secretly worried that the vibration of the engine would eventually cajole the insecure belt off its wheels. But maybe – just maybe – it would hold until Kalgoorlie.

The rotor arm was less of a problem. It slotted perfectly into the distributor cap. When I spun it with my fingers it managed to twirl without difficulty – but that still didn't guarantee it would fire the engine. I clipped the cap back into place, ran back to the cab and ripped out a handful of wires beneath the steering wheel. Within minutes, I'd found the two necessary wires, cut them in half with a pocket knife and shaved away the plastic coating at each of their edges.

It was moment-of-truth time. I sat up at the wheel, threw the stick shift to neutral, pumped the gas pedal twice, sucked in my breath and touched the exposed wires together. Nothing.

I found the choke and pulled it out a notch. Another pump of the gas pedal. Another deep breath before the wires met again. Nothing.

Krystal, standing by the open hood, shook her head. No movement at all within the engine.

Fuck up, fuck up.

I ordered myself to stay calm and jerked the choke all the way out, but kept my foot off the gas. This time, I struck the wires against each other, as if I was lighting a match. And there was . . .

A rumble. Brief and low – but a rumble nonetheless.

Now the choke went back to the halfway point and the wires were struck twice without pause.

A *protracted* rumble.

My foot depressed the pedal ever so slightly. Wires.

Brrmmmmmmmmmmmmmmmmmmmmmmmmmmmmmmm.

I pumped the gas madly, trying to sustain the blast of ignition. For a moment, it looked like it was about to die again, but I readjusted the choke to low, put the pedal to the floor and listened as the engine finally lurched out of hesitancy and clicked into lift-off.

Krystal banged the hood shut and looked out over the rim of the plateau, scanning the scene below.

'They're on the road,' she yelled, before running back to the cab and climbing in beside me. 'Go.'

I slammed the stick shift into first, released the clutch and waited for the almighty heave that would finally get us on the road. Instead, the front wheels started making telltale grinding sounds. Something was bogging us down, impeding our way. Leaving the motor still running, we both jumped out and saw that the wheels were blocked by several bloated 'roo corpses. With no spade or shovel – and no time for revulsion – we had to use our hands to dig them away. Then it was back to the cab, clutch down, stick shift in first, pedal to the metal, a moment of silent prayer before . . .

The sucker finally moved. With one big belch of a lurch, we started budging forward, the craggy topography of the plateau making the lorry pitch and sway. It took ten jolting minutes to cross this tableland and connect up with the road heading west. But my relief at seeing the start of this one-lane route soon disappeared when I discovered that it was impossible to accelerate beyond 20 mph. For this unpaved track was another continuous horror show of small dips and cavities – the kind of surface that might just be negotiable with a small four-wheel-drive, but was insane to tackle with an old lumbering tank. Every few yards we slammed into some new hollow, some minor crater.

'When does it get better?' I asked Krystal.

'It doesn't.'

'Jesus. How far to the main road?'

'Around four hundred kilometres.'

'That's twelve hours from here at this speed.' I could hear the panic in my voice.

'I know,' Krystal said quietly.

'And they're only . . . what? . . . thirty, forty minutes behind us?'

'Just keep driving.'

'We're goners.'

'Fourteen hours and we're in Kalgoorlie.'

'A *mere* fourteen hours . . .'

'Buy you a beer when we get there.'

'You'll buy me two,' I said. 'And a shower. I'd kill now for some hot water and soap.'

'Might even buy us a motel room for the night.'

'You're on . . . and I'll take care of the air tickets.'

'Where to?'

'Boston.'

Silence.

'You mean that?' she said.

'Yeah. I mean that.'

'I don't know . . .'

'You do.'

'But . . .'

'Won't take no.'

'But . . .'

'Won't take "but" either.'

She never once turned to look at me, keeping her gaze fixed on the road ahead of us, remaining silent for what seemed like an hour. Then finally said: 'Okay. Boston.'

'Good,' I said.

'I'd better like it there.'

'If you don't, then we'll get into a car and go somewhere else. The road's full of possibilities.'

We hit another pothole.

'Not this road,' Krystal said.

The sun showed up an hour later. With it came ruthless heat. It turned the cab into a sweat-box. It scorched our throats. It made us desperate for water.

'I'm sure there's a little running stream an hour or so beyond here,' Krystal said.

'Hope you're right – 'cause we're dead without it.'

She *was* right – only it took more than three hours to reach it. Three hours through arid khaki-coloured tableland, with not a speck of shade in sight. Three hours at a speed so sluggish that I really came to believe we were going nowhere fast. Daddy couldn't be far behind.

But then Krystal shouted, '*There*!' And there indeed it was: a tiny rivulet of water cascading across the road. It was only about a foot deep, but we stopped the lorry and fell into it as if it was a deep cool lake. The water tasted a little metallic. Neither of us complained. With only a few minutes to spare, we drank like idiots, filled Krystal's canteen, then washed away all the 'roo blood and dirt. I almost felt clean.

'How far to the next stream?' I asked.

'Maybe another three hours.'

We stood motionless for a moment, trying to discern the hum of another vehicle in the distance.

Not a sound.

'We might just get there,' I said.

For a little while, the road smoothed out and I was able to crank up the lorry to a nippy 35 mph. But then we were back in the topographical doldrums, pitching and rolling, terrified that every pothole might just snap the fan-belt.

We didn't say much – because we were both concentrating so hard on the road itself (Krystal gluing herself to the windscreen and barking out red alerts of obstacles up ahead). Being pursued by somebody with a gun also tends to stifle small talk, and every ten miles or so we'd stop for a moment so Krystal could dash out a few yards behind the lorry and to listen again for the drone of a stalking van.

But all she could hear was the hush of the bush.

After three hours, the midday sun was at full brutish throttle, Krystal's canteen was empty again, there was still no sign of the stream, and I was beginning to wonder what it must be like to die of thirst. Because nothing I had ever encountered before could match the cruelty of the terrain we had now entered. We were in an unbroken plane of sand. No hills, no knolls, no trees, no shade, not even a scrubby bit of Spinifex. Nothing lived here, because this was a wasteland that killed any organism which strayed into its enormity. An arid world rendered flat. Blood-red. Molten. The dead heart of the continent.

Another hour and another hour. *Where's the fucking stream?* I glanced over at Krystal. Her stint at the windscreen had left her sunstruck, wilted, drained. At least the road had flattened out for a stretch, allowing her a respite from scouting for obstacles. I, too, was wrung-out, parched, starting to feel the first threatening tingles of delirium. We needed water fast.

And five minutes later we drove right over it.

It wasn't a stream. It wasn't even a rivulet; more of a negligible trickle – just deep enough to fill a canteen. We sat down in it, cupped our hands and guzzled.

'You're gonna have to buy me three beers in Kalgoorlie,' I eventually said.

'I'll buy you as many as you can down.'

I put my arms around her and let her head slump against my shoulder. Exhaustion hit us both so badly that we didn't move for a few minutes. Didn't hear the van approach. Didn't look up until Daddy fired a shot in the air to let us know we were cornered.

The van was only a few hundred yards behind us, closing in fast. Les was at the wheel. Daddy had his rifle pointed out the side window and let go with another two shots above our heads. They sent us scrambling for the cab – but when we tried to climb in, a third shot slammed into the roof of the lorry. We dived for cover, cowering by the radiator grille.

'Get the fuck out,' Daddy yelled. I peered out the side. The van was now bearing down on us, Les cranking it up to maximum speed. I glanced at Krystal. She looked very afraid.

'What do we do?' I hissed.

'What can we do?' she said. 'They've got us.'

But just as we were about to step into the road with our hands up, there was a terrific clang. The speeding van hit a pothole and flipped over on its left side. Daddy went flying on top of Les. They screamed at each other. Loudly.

We made a dash for the cab. The engine was still running. With another heave, we got the lorry moving again. I put the pedal to the floor, but we still couldn't top 20 mph. Krystal turned around in her seat and gave me a running commentary as Daddy and Les finally scrambled out of their van and tried to right it again.

'Looks like they're not hurt . . . think they're having problems pushing it . . . doesn't want to budge . . . Daddy's yelling something at Les . . . now he's shaking him by the shoulders, telling him off, kicking a fender . . . they're trying again . . . Daddy's got his back up against a door, Les is shoving with his hands . . . nah, it's still not moving . . . they're stuck . . . the bastards are stuck . . .'

I laughed a manic laugh. I couldn't believe our luck. Especially when I peered into the rearview mirror and saw Daddy running after us, rifle in hand, eventually staggering to a halt, firing a useless shot in the air, panting for breath in the desert sun, screaming something incoherent, his rage bellowing out across the empty sand. Then the lorry hit a downward slope and he was gone. Left stranded on the high ground above us.

We entered a deep valley – the lorry gaining speed as it rolled down into a desolate canyon. The crimson sand turned into brown grit – the earth so dry that it was fractured, eerie fissures cracking the land. There were animal bones everywhere. There was nothing else in sight.

'Next water is at the main road,' Krystal finally said. 'We get stuck before then . . .' Her voice trailed off. She craned her neck to look behind us. 'You think they'll get it moving again?' she asked.

'I don't know.'

'If they don't, they're dead.'

She said nothing else for a very long time. Just stared out the window, sad beyond comfort. Then: 'We have to go back.'

'No way,' I said.

'They'll die.'

'They'll kill us.'

'It's my father, my uncle . . .'

'They shot at us.'

'They won't if we go back. They'll be grateful.'

'Grateful to you, not to me. They'll shoot me like they shot Jack. Remember Jack?'

Krystal's head snapped back, as if I'd slapped her across the face.

'I'm sorry,' I said.

She put her hand to her mouth and started to sob. I stopped the lorry, put my arms around her. She buried her head on my shoulder and cried. I stroked her hair. I kept saying how sorry, dumb, stupid I was. I felt like the biggest shit on earth.

And when I turned away for a moment, I glanced into the rearview and saw it. The van. Racing towards us at speed. Immediately, I broke off the embrace, hit the accelerator and tried to get us moving. But Les was too fast for us. He roared off the track, passed us in the sand, then pulled the van across our path. As soon as he braked, Daddy jumped out and trained his rifle on me.

'Out, right now,' he ordered.

I brought the lorry to a halt. I looked at Krystal. She nodded her head. We climbed out of the cab and stood together in front of the hood. When she took my hand, Daddy's eyes widened with rage.

'You Yank-wank,' he said. 'Thought you left us to die back there, didn't you?'

'Daddy –' Krystal said.

'Shut up, you,' he said, pulling back the hammer of the gun. 'Screwing around behind my Princess's back . . .'

'We didn't screw around . . .' I pleaded.

He raised the gun again. Krystal became distraught. 'Daddy, no!' she yelled.

He ignored her and pointed the barrel at me. This can't be happening, this *can't* . . .

'All right, all right,' I said, sounding distraught too. 'I'll go back. Never try to run again. Do whatever you –'

'You're going nowhere, fuckwit.' He now had the barrel aimed at my heart.

'Hang on, now, Daddy,' Les said.

His finger moved to the trigger.

'We'll take him back to Wollanup,' Les said, 'kick the shit out of him. But not this, mate. You can't do this again.'

'Fuck I can't.'

I glanced around frantically. Nowhere to run. He was smiling at me. The bastard was smiling at me while his fucking finger was tightening around the trigger. And I heard myself screaming . . . '*Nooooooooooooooooooooooooooooooo*' . . . before I jumped away and the gun went off.

After the blast, came silence. An eerie, dazed silence as I lay on the ground, face-first in the sand. A silence broken by a cry. An animal-like wail. Soul-sick. Inconsolable. From Daddy.

Then I looked up and saw Krystal.

Staggering towards me. Her T-shirt soaked in blood. Her face filled with disbelief.

'Oh, shit,' she whispered. 'Oh, shit.'

Before I could reach her, she crumpled and lay very still. Daddy dropped the gun and came charging – scooping her up in his arms, rocking her back and forth, his sobbing uncontrollable. Les was now by his side, Krystal's left wrist in his hand as he felt for a pulse. After a moment, he let it go, dropped to his knees and put his face in his hands.

I was beyond shock. I was operating on some deranged auto-pilot. My brain reeling. My legs like rubber, as I lurched over to the spot where Daddy had dropped his gun. I picked it up. I cocked the hammer. I pointed the barrel at my father-in-law and roared his name.

'*Millard*!'

He dropped Krystal and lunged for me – his nostrils flared like a bull, his eyes crazed. I fired twice. And caught him twice. In the face. As Daddy fell backwards, Les let out a howl. But when he tried to stand up, I trained the rifle on him.

'Don't fucking move,' I said.

'Please, mate . . .' he said, his voice weak, diminished.

I pulled back the hammer. Les began to cry, begging me not to shoot him, his body shaking, the fear raw. I smashed the barrel of the rifle across his face. He doubled-over.

'Get up,' I said. I could feel the gun trembling in my hands.

He put his hands over his head, his cries now hysterical. I kicked him. First in the stomach. Then in the teeth. Logic had fled the scene. I really wanted to kill him.

'I said, get the fuck up.' I was screaming.

He somehow made it to his feet. His nose and mouth were haemorrhaging blood. I ordered him to put his hands behind his head and walk to the van. When he got there, I made him stand face-front against the vehicle. Then I kicked his legs apart and frisked him. Two hundred bucks in cash. Car keys. I pocketed both.

'Turn around,' I said.

As soon as he faced me, he fell to his knees and started sobbing again, pleading with me to spare him. I tried to figure out my next move.

Finally, I said, 'Put Krystal in the back of the lorry.'

Still shaking, he hesitated for a moment. When I shouted, 'Do it now!' he stumbled over to her body, put his arms under her shoulders and legs, and gently lifted her up. I had to shut my eyes as he carried her to the lorry. I didn't want to see her face.

'Get Daddy in beside her.'

It took some effort, but Les was just about big enough to drag Daddy over and hoist him aboard.

'Now, climb into the cab. The driver's seat.'

He did as commanded. I slid in next to him and let the rifle nuzzle his head. The engine was still humming away. 'Turn it around,' I said.

Instantly, he had it backed up, then shoved it into first and drove in a semicircle around the van, pointing it back towards Wollanup.

'How much gas you got in the van?' I said.

'Half a tank – and there's a full jerry-can of petrol in the back.'

'How far to the main road?'

'Two hours, no more.'

'You gonna try to follow me?'

'No way. Promise.'

'If you do, I will kill you. Understand?'

He nodded. Many times.

'I *should* kill you.'

More sobbing.

'Shift back to neutral,' I said. 'And keep both hands on the wheel until I tell you to move 'em.'

I grabbed my day-pack off the floor and climbed slowly out of the cab. As I backed away from the lorry, I kept the rifle pointed at him. 'Get on home now,' I said.

His voice was barely a mutter. 'I'm . . . sorry. I'm . . .'

'Fuck you all,' I said. 'Now move.'

He drove off. I stood in the centre of the road – finger still on the trigger – and waited until the lorry had dissolved into the horizon. Then I climbed into the van and spent several minutes clutching the wheel so hard that my knuckles almost ruptured the skin. Sucker-punch horror: KO'd by what I'd seen, what I'd done. The heat of the cab finally snapped me out of it. I turned the key in the ignition and drove over two fading puddles of blood. Ten minutes ago, the blood wasn't there. Now the sun had dried it out so thoroughly it was already merging with the red of the sand.

Two hours later, I did meet the main road. It was a single

lane of blacktop, empty of traffic. Before turning on to it, I left the van – day-pack in hand – and stripped off everything I was wearing and washed myself down in the tiny trickle of water that ran by the road. After changing into my spare set of clothes, I used a capful of petrol from the jerry-can to douse my blood-splattered shirt and shorts, then dropped a match on the pile. While they burned, I walked out a few hundred yards into the desert and buried the rifle. Now, if any cop stopped me, I wouldn't be a man fleeing a homicide (with all the evidence needed to implicate him). Just a dumb American tourist who'd got lost driving the back roads of the bush.

But no cop stopped me – because I didn't encounter another car all the way to Kalgoorlie. En route I had to pull over several times when my hands shook so much that I thought I might lose control of the van. It was eight by the time I saw a faint hint of city lights in the night sky. I sidestepped the town and drove straight to the airport. In the parking lot, I used an old rag to wipe down the steering-wheel, the dash, the door handles and every other conceivable part of the vehicle I might have touched. Then I walked into the terminal and bought a seat on the last flight out to Perth that night.

'That'll be one hundred and thirty-nine dollars one way,' said the woman at the ticket desk, 'but I can do you a cheap return for one hundred and seventy-nine.'

'No thanks,' I said. 'I'm not coming back.'

I paid cash. As I handed it over, I could see her studying my face with care. Was it *that* obvious? Did she suss me? Had word already gone out – an All Points Bulletin on an American, wanted for homicide, believed to be in the Kalgoorlie area? As soon as she issued this ticket, she'd probably duck into a back office and call the cops. The bitch is gonna shop me. Get her picture in the paper and ten minutes of local fame for sending me up the river. A twenty-year stretch in some Australian big house. Could smash your face in, you fucking bitch. Could . . .

'Boarding through Gate Six in twenty minutes. Have a nice flight, sir.'

I grunted thanks, grabbed the ticket, bolted for the toilet and hid in a cubicle. When I stopped trembling, I filled a sink with cold water and plunged my head into it, holding it under until I gasped.

Chill the fuck out. There's no way anybody knows anything. The bodies are en route back to Wollanup. Nobody ever drives that road – because it's now off the map. And nobody in Wollanup is going to say anything, because that will mean the end of Wollanup. You've gotten away with it. You've *walked*. You're on your way out of here.

The flight was empty. I sat in the back of the fifty-seat turbo-prop, and chased four scotches with four beers during the seventy minutes we were cruising. At Perth Airport, there was a long line of taxis outside the terminal building. I was the only customer.

'What's the best hotel in town?' I asked the cabbie at the front of the line.

'The Hilton, I guess.'

'Let's go.'

Halfway there, an old Beatles song came over the cab's radio. And as Paul McCartney sang 'She's Leaving Home', I lost a fight I had been waging for the past couple of hours.

'Y'orright, mate?' the cabbie asked. I was crying so hard I couldn't answer him. 'Easy now, mate,' the cabbie said. 'Ain't the end of the world, is it?'

'Shut up,' I whispered.

I somehow managed to regain my composure by the time we reached the Hilton. It was located off William Street, right in the middle of downtown. The streets were abandoned. Perth was out cold for the night. And the fussy little clerk behind the registration desk didn't like the look of me.

'All our standard rooms are fully booked,' he said, his tone dismissive.

'You've got absolutely nothing?'

'Just a suite at three hundred and twenty-five dollars a night.'

I slapped down my Visa card and said, 'Sold.'

'I see,' he said, taken aback. 'I'm afraid I am first going to have to get credit approval from Visa.'

'You do that.'

He disappeared for a few minutes, then came back all smiles. Plastic money buys you the most spurious form of respect.

'Everything's just fine, Mr Hawthorne. Shall I have the porter bring up your bags?'

'This is my bag,' I said, pointing to the day-pack. He worked hard at remaining nonplussed.

'Anything we can get you, sir?'

'Toothbrush, toothpaste, shaving gear.'

'You *are* travelling light,' he said.

'May I have the fucking key. Please.'

'Very good, sir.'

The suite was a Louis XIV playpen – all rococo furniture and gold leaf and a bed the size of a football field. I undressed, put on the hotel bathrobe, and handed my dirty laundry to the porter who brought up the toiletries. He promised to have everything washed and pressed by morning.

Then I stepped into the shower. Proper hot water. Stinging needlepoint pressure. I didn't leave it for a half-hour. There was a lot to wash away.

I was too tired to eat. I climbed in between the frosty, stiff sheets, poured myself a miniature of Scotch from the mini-bar and was asleep within minutes.

No spooky nocturnal visions. No flashback atrocities. Not even a benign dream. A seamless night. The true sleep of the dead. When I finally stirred, I enjoyed a few minutes of gentle befuddlement before the horror hit. Angie. The chicken coop. Dead 'roos. Daddy. Krystal. Especially Krystal.

You mean that? she had asked when I proposed Boston.

Yeah, I mean that, I'd said – and for the first time in my life, I had.

How do you live with a chronic ache? You just do, I guess. You just get through the day. And you start now.

I ordered a mammoth breakfast. I took another long shower. I changed into my fresh-laundered clothes. I visited the hotel barber and had nine months of tangled hair clipped away. I settled the bill. I walked through the high-rise canyon of downtown Perth and encountered the first stop-light I had seen since leaving Darwin. I entered American Express and reported the accidental loss of $6500 in traveller's cheques. The clerk's eyes grew wide when she heard the sum. I handed over the refund slip. There were phone calls to head office in Sydney. There was an hour's wait while the computer corroborated all my serial numbers. There were forms to fill out and a short lecture from the clerk about keeping traveller's cheques safe in the future. But eventually the money was refunded, and I walked out of the Amex office, amazed that Les had never cashed any of the cheques I'd been forced to sign over. Until I saw a board listing rates of exchange. Since disappearing into Wollanup, the US dollar had lost almost 50 per cent of its value against the Aussie dollar. The greedy bastard had apparently decided not to deposit my cheques until the US rate improved.

My next stop was a travel agency. I handed over my airline ticket and asked to be booked on the next plane to London, with an immediate onward connection to Boston. She punched numbers into a computer and gave me some bad news: there was a flight leaving at 4.45 that afternoon, but it was already full in economy.

'Book me into Business Class,' I said.

'It's an additional one thousand, three hundred and seventy-five dollars, sir.'

Once again, the Visa card came cracking down on a countertop.

'Do it,' I said.

I sat in a darkened bar for the next few hours, nursing a few beers, laying low, killing time. Around three that afternoon, I asked the barkeep to call me a taxi to the airport. Thirty minutes later, I was checked in and en route to the Business Class lounge, where I planned to hide out until the final boarding call for my flight. But first I had to pass through the immigration checkpoint.

The inspector was a gaunt man in his fifties with a plastic pen holder – a nerd pack – in his breast pocket. He snapped his fingers for my passport, scrutinized me with his glacial civil servant eyes, then spent a long time staring at the picture in my travel document. I watched as he licked his forefinger every time he turned a page, finally stopping when he reached my Australian visa and entry stamps. His eyes narrowed, his thin lips tightened, he turned back to the first page, looked at my photograph again, and shot me another chilling glance. Then he stood up from his desk and said, 'Wait here, please.'

I tried to sound as calm as possible, but I could already feel my palms succumbing to sweat.

'Anything wrong?' I asked, my voice weak.

'Yes,' he said and briskly walked off down a corridor.

When he returned, five minutes later, he was accompanied by two men: an angular senior inspector-type in a dark suit, and a uniformed airport policeman. I turned white, felt feeble, felt dead. They *knew*. Somehow they'd found out. Maybe Les didn't make it back to Wollanup, but instead headed for Kalgoorlie, raised the alarm, and told the cops that I had shot Daddy *and* Krystal. How would I ever get out of that one . . . or explain the last nine months? And even if the authorities did believe me, they'd still make me pay for Daddy's death. Would they buy a plea of self-defence? Probably . . . and then sentence me to reduced time. A mere ten years. I'm gonna be stuck in this fucking country until I'm fifty? No way, no way. Please, oh, please, just let me on that plane and I promise – swear in blood – you'll never see me here again.

Mr Dark Suit had my passport in his hand.

'Mr . . .' he opened the cover, stared at my name '. . . Hawthorne. Nicholas Thomas Hawthorne?'

'Is there some sort of problem?' I asked.

'You will come with us, please.'

'But why . . .?'

The uniformed cop was now at my back. He tapped me with his forefinger.

'This way, sir.'

Mr Dark Suit led the way, the cop brought up the rear; I was sandwiched between them. We marched down three corridors and entered a rabbit warren of offices with frosted glass doors. Mr Dark Suit opened one with a key, turned on the fluorescent light, motioned me to sit in a straight-back metal chair while he placed himself behind a metal desk. The cop stood at the door.

'Now, Mr . . . Hawthorne,' Mr Dark Suit said. 'I suppose you realize why you are here?'

I said nothing and kept my gaze fixed on the scuffed lino floor. Mr Dark Suit got testy.

'Please answer the question. Do you understand why you are being detained?'

'Yes, sir.'

'You understand that you have broken the law, committed a serious offence?'

A shudder ran through me and I had to squeeze my hands into fists to avoid shaking.

'Under Australian law, you can have counsel present at this interview. But it would expedite matters if you would agree to answer some questions straight away. Will you co-operate?'

I nodded my consent.

'Good,' Mr Dark Suit said and pulled a set of forms out of a desk drawer.

'Now, Mr Hawthorne, will you please explain to me . . . why you have overstayed your visitor's visa by six months?'

I blinked in disbelief and heard myself saying, '*What* . . .?'

'You entered Darwin nine months and three days ago on a Class Six-Seventy Visitor's Visa which, though valid for multiple travel over a calendar year, still only permits you temporary entry to Australia for a period of three months at a time. But you have overstayed this entry visa by six months and three days . . . which means you have violated Australian Immigration law.'

The penny was starting to drop. *Play dumb, play dumb,* I told myself.

'So that's why you're detaining me now?' I asked, trying to sound a little slow on the uptake. Mr Dark Suit grew testier.

'Yes, Mr Hawthorne, it's how the Immigration law works here. If you overstay your visa, you are detained upon departure. Now would you mind explaining why you didn't attempt to apply for an extension of your entry visa?'

I played very dumb. I said I'd never read the small print on the visa and thought it was good for a year. Mr Dark Suit told me I should have known better. I said I was an inexperienced traveller – as my empty passport showed, Australia was my first overseas visit in years. Then he bombarded me with questions. About my profession, about why I was travelling for so long, about where I had visited ('Darwin, the Kimberley, then I camped around Broome for a couple of months'). Was I going back to a job? ('The Akron Ohio *Beacon Journal* expects me to start next Monday'). Did I buy any property here? Did I ever do any paid work while I'd been in Australia? He appeared satisfied with my answers, and even seemed to buy my naïve tourist act. But there was one final hurdle to clear. Mr Dark Suit picked up the phone and called the state and federal police.

'Hawthorne, Nicholas Thomas; US Passport number L8713142. Any ongoing inquiries?'

Minutes passed. Finally, Mr Dark Suit muttered, 'I see,' replaced the receiver, and glared at me. 'The police . . . have no interest in questioning you.'

I had to work hard at suppressing my relief.

'But we are still entitled to detain you – and, in fact, arrest you for breach of Immigration laws. Unless, of course, you agree to voluntary repatriation.'

'What does that mean?'

'You sign a form admitting that you overstayed your entry permit, and you agree not to apply for an Australian visa for thirty-six months – as you will be barred from entering the country during this time.'

'Where do I sign?' I said.

After the paperwork was completed, I was held in the interview room until the final call for my flight. The uniformed cop escorted me to the gate. The lounge was empty. I was the last passenger and the ground staff were waiting for me. The cop handed me back my passport and my boarding card.

'Obey the rules next time, sir,' he said, 'and your departure from Australia will be an easier one.'

I wanted to say – *Ever heard of Wollanup rules, mate?* – but held myself back. I had to get on that plane.

They checked my boarding card, they checked my passport, they escorted me down the airbridge, they brought me to a big overstuffed seat and handed me a glass of champagne. As the 747 taxied out, I kept thinking: the plane will come to a sudden stop on the tarmac, we will return to the terminal, and I will be rearrested. Because I am guilty. Guilty of so much.

But the plane kept edging its way to the runway. And then we were airborne. Within minutes, the city was gone, the land was red.

More champagne. I settled back in my seat. Once I paid off the credit card, I'd have more than $4,000 to play with. Enough to make a start again. Not to Akron and the job offer I left behind. No dead ends this time, no cul-de-sacs of my own making. And no more reckless drifting. I had spent my life chasing the transitory, dodging any obligation or involvement that might have challenged me. I'd been a free agent, so alone in the world that no one even knew I had vanished for nine months. No one cared. Except Krystal – and she cared too much. Because I wasn't worth the price she paid. And now here I was, a free agent again. Not a tie to bind me – and finally terrified of my solitude, my rootlessness. Who said, a life without commitment is a life without substance? Some sanctimonious schmuck, no doubt . . . yet the guy had his finger on the truth.

Three more glasses of champagne and I nodded off. For hours. A scene danced across my shuddered eyes. I am a man of sixty – a retired teacher, living quietly in a little house in a little Maine seaport. It is winter. Snow is falling. I am sitting by the fire in the living-room, reading a magazine, sipping the first whisky of the evening. A knock comes at the door. I answer it. Outside is a kid around twenty – hair to his shoulders, a backpack slung over one arm, a bush hat covered with snow. His face is my face. But his accent is pure Oz.

'*G'day, Dad,*' he says.

Out of the shadows behind him steps a bloated woman in her early forties, her blonde hair gone prematurely grey. She smiles a malevolent smile. There are only three teeth left in her mouth. The kid throws his arm around her.

'*And say g'day to Mum . . .*'

I felt a hand on my shoulder, shaking me hard.

'Sir, sir, *sir.*'

I snapped back awake. An air hostess was standing over me, looking very worried.

'You've been screaming,' she said.

'Really?'

'Very loud.'

'Oh.'

'Are you all right?'

'I'm . . . fine.'

She gave me a big white smile. And said, 'You must've had a nightmare.'

Is that what they call it?